THE RUSSIAN HIT
MICHELLE WISHART

Table of Contents

My first novel in the Roxxy Foxx Series, The Russian Hit, is dedicated to my husband, Andy.

Andy, you are my rock. Your unwavering encouragement and support have got me through every aspect of this adventure.

Thank you, my love.

As always,

Lucky me

BELL'S PUBLISHING CO, LLC.

THE RUSSIAN HIT

BELL'S PUBLISHING CO, LLC

514 America's Way #16467

Box Elder, SD 57719

<u>bellspublishingco@gmail.com</u>

Published in the United States by

Bells Publishing CO

ISBN: 978-1-7369014-0-3

E-ISBN: 978-1-7369014-1-0

Prologue

MY NAME IS ROXXANNE Foxx, but I go by Roxxy. I am five foot eight inches with straight dark auburn (pain in my ass, thick as horsehair) hair down to my waist and light green eyes of Irish descent. My Granny and Poppy raised me since I was eight years old when my parents died in a car accident.

I'm a retired US Air Force Captain, and I was assigned as a Security Forces Sniper, which helped me land a job with Folsom State Prison. After sniper school, the Correctional Officer Academy was a cakewalk. Oh, shock! My specialty was, you guessed it, winner-winner chicken dinner, a "Sniper" Most of the time, I worked in the guard tower watching the COs six whenever they were in the yard. Not to brag or anything, but I can shoot the ass off a gnat at fifteen hundred meters, and that is where my talents end.

About a year ago, I was terminated for punching my superior officer. I'm usually a by-the-book kind of girl until I lose my Irish temper. The turd had it coming, and I don't feel bad about it in the least. It's not like I invited the skeeze to grab my ass.

These days I do PI work in my hometown of Sacramento, California. I've lived in Sacramento my whole life, except when I was off saving the world with my highly trained, extremely unprofessional talents with the USAF. I now permanently live in Sacramento Midtown, better known as the Lavender District, nicknamed by the gay community who live in the area, famous for its restaurants, breweries, and nightclubs.

I inherited my Grandma Bessie's Victorian. Otherwise, I would never be able to afford to live in Midtown. Not without selling my cars and bikes. Some girls collect shoes; I collect cars, bikes, and maybe guns. While I was in the military, I always chose to live on base or I was on assignment, so I didn't have much in the way of financial obligations. What can I say? I collected a few cars and a couple of bikes or four. Luckily, there's a large carriage house at the back of Granny's house, accessible through the alley with two two-car, extra-deep garages and two extra-deep carport bays.

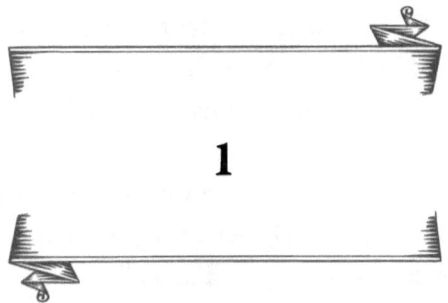

1

ON DAYS LIKE THIS, I wonder how I got myself into this mess. I'm on day three of four-day surveillance. I'm in a flat Black Town and Country minivan. Usually, I wouldn't say I like minivans; my nickname for them is Moron-van. You can guess why. This particular minivan is pretty bitchin'. It's the perfect surveillance rig. After negotiating a sweet deal, I took it to my buddy's place and had all

the windows completely blacked out. You can't even see shadows through the windows. Then I took a picture of the interior, looking from the front window to the back of the van. I transferred the image onto the material to make a partition, and it seems like the van is empty. Clever, right? I took the middle-row seats out and installed a mini-fridge and a Porta-potty. It sucks to lose a mark because you had to pee in the middle of surveillance. Anyway, this is my third day on surveillance for this crazy lady. She hired me to see if her geeky husband was cheating on her. What a snooze-ville. He leaves for work precisely at seven a.m. He goes to the dentist's office located at Broadway and Fifteenth Street. I watch for him to sneak away all day. At the end of each day, he leaves precisely at five o'clock and drives straight home, using the same route each day.

Unless he's boinking the dental hygienists on the exam chair between the steady stream of appointments, he's not doing anything. He doesn't go anywhere other than straight to work and straight home. It's the most boring surveillance I've ever worked on. He must be a great dentist to have so many patients come to this crappy neighborhood to see him. I have all the hookers and Johns to watch to pass the time. John pulls to the curb, the hooker jumps in, and they go around the corner. Five minutes later, the hooker strolls back to the corner, popping a fresh piece of gum in her mouth, Yuck! Did I mention it was a crappy neighborhood?

Day four was the same, except the temperature went up about fifteen degrees. I was sweating more than a whore in church. At five o'clock, the dentist closed the shop, and the dentist and the receptionist walked to their respective cars without saying a word. It's kind of weird, not even a "Good night" or "Have a nice weekend" the body language is not one of which they are having an affair but more of submissive nature.

I could see why Mrs. Fruit Basket Dentist would be jealous. The receptionist is hot. She's skinny but has an excellent boob job, her platinum blond hair cut in an A-line bob framing her flawless ivory face.

Each day I saw the two of them leave simultaneously but never together. Little Ms. Platinum must have a closet full of sleeveless turtlenecks. All four days, four assorted colors. Who wears turtleneck sweaters (sleeveless or not) in the middle of summer?

I followed the dentist at a comfortable distance and kept driving past the house; as he pulled into his driveway, I saw the garage door open.

Tomorrow is Friday, and I will meet with Ms. Coo Coo Cachoo Dentist, and give her the disturbing news, her husband is the most boring man alive. He doesn't even stop to pop back a beer or two.

I park my work van at a parking structure a few blocks from home. I don't want the spy rig associated with my house. The PI business comes with a lot of fruitcakes. I parked the spy rig in its usual assigned parking space and backed into one side of the parking space next to the concrete wall.

I had the doors to the van locked while I was sitting there a moment longer to enjoy the air conditioner for a minute before walking the few blocks home in the scorching hot temperature.

Suddenly, my spidey senses started creeping, and then it was a full-on five alarms yelling at me. I learned a long time ago to listen. It saved my ass and my team's ass on more than one occasion. I scooched in my seat just as a black SUV slowly rolled up, lowering the backseat window, the passenger leveling a fully automatic weapon at me. Everything slowed down as he opened fire on me. I rolled between the seats and got to the back of the van, grabbing my Poppy's Desert Eagle 50 cal, which I kept in a holster I fastened to the back of the driver seat. I popped the back hatch, using the van as a barrier, returning fire. In the distance, I can hear sirens. The cavalry is on the way. The black SUV hauled ass; I ran out from behind my van, putting three more rounds into the back of the SUV. I hit the driver in the back of the head. The SUV was still moving at a high rate of speed, careening into parked cars, finally coming to a stop on its side. The sirens were getting closer, and the guy from the back seat climbed out the side window, throwing a couple of rounds toward the approaching police car as he ran away. I set my weapon on the ground, raised my hands, and waited for the police officers to clear the overturned SUV. Within a few minutes, the entire parking garage was swarming with police. I was promptly handcuffed and placed in the backseat of a patrol car.

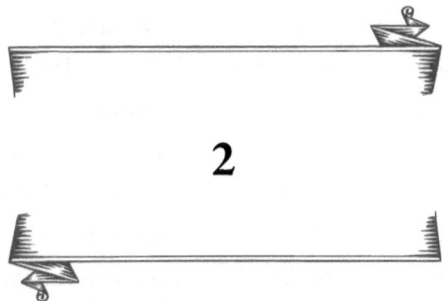

2

ABOUT AN HOUR LATER, a fine-ass detective named Connolly came to the cruiser to drill me with his questions, and all I could think about was wanting him to drill me in other ways. I gave him a detailed statement of what happened. He asked if I recognized any of the men who attacked me. I said, "I have no clue who they are or why they wanted to kill me, but I have made some enemies over my lifetime. It can be related to my military background or my CO position at Folsom Prison. I didn't even get a good look at the guy who ran off, except at this distance, he looked kind of small, and he was white." He said, "What about the PI work you do? Could it have been related to an investigation?" I laughed and said, "I do adulterous spouses, missing persons, background checks, all incredibly humdrum stuff." Connolly said, going over his notes, "You said you scooched down in your seat? How did you know what was about to happen? Did someone warn you?" I said, "No, my spidey sense told me." He smiled the biggest, most gorgeous smile and gave the slightest head shake, so little it was hardly noticeable. He asked, "If I heard of Igor Stanlogovich?" I shook my head and said, "No clue. Is it the dead guy?" Showing me the I.D. in a plastic evidence bag. He said, "It's the name on the driver's license from his pocket, he doesn't have a face to match the picture, so hopefully, his prints are in the system."

I shrugged and said, "Sorry (not sorry), I like big guns with a heavy load in my rounds." I turned to look at the spy rig. I was amazed I was still standing there in one piece, breathing. I chuckled. Connolly cocked his head to one side, looking at me like I was batshit crazy.

He said, "What?" I smiled and said, "They were shitty shooters. Whoever hired them should get a refund." He said, "Hired?" I said, "Yeah, obviously someone hired them. I don't recognize the guy on the I.D. or the little guy who ran off. I would remember any man that small. Also, I would know anyone who disliked me enough to put this number of rounds in me." He asked, "How do you think they found you here?" "I think they followed me today; I would have known if it was any longer than today." I said, "So, you don't think they know where you live?" He asked.

I said, "I have thought about that too and replayed all the cars parked in my neighborhood over the last few days." He raised an eyebrow and said: "How would you remember parked cars?" "I have an eidetic memory. If I see it, I remember it. It's a gift and a burden. Since I started doing PI work, I have parked here so that no one could associate my work car with my house. There are a lot of fruit loops in the PI business, both with clients and marks. I live a few blocks from here, and my house is in my Granny's family name."

We were at the scene for hours, and finally, when both vehicles were on flatbed tow trucks wrapped in yellow CSI tarps on the way to the impound to be processed, Connolly offered to give me a lift home. I graciously accepted; I was suddenly exhausted. Also, my weapon was now in evidence, so I didn't want to go home after this evening's events without being armed. I asked if he wouldn't mind clearing my house for me before he left, not that I needed him to clear my house. I thought he should pay particularly close attention to my bedroom. Then I smiled to myself for being naughty after the day I had. I must be okay, a little bent, but okay. It was after midnight by the time Connolly cleared the house, and he ensured that no one tampered with the carriage house. After he said good night, I set the security alarm as he left. I fell into bed, thinking about the hot Detective Connolly. I almost had sex with myself but rolled over and slept long and hard.

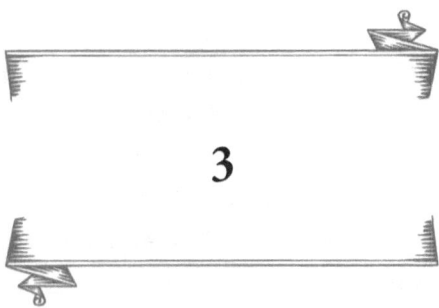

3

I LOVE FRIDAYS! I make it a habit of taking Fridays off, except with an occasional invoice and picking up payment. Today I'm going to meet with Mrs. Crazy Dentist to report precisely how boring her husband is and to submit my invoice for payment. Then I might take a nice ride out Jackson Highway to Ione to the Sacramento Valley Gun Range. After yesterday I should brush up with my handguns. Usually, this is where I go with my long gun, but today, I feel like riding my motorcycle, and it might be a bit conspicuous riding down Jackson Highway with an M-24 sniper rifle strapped to my back. I think I'll ride "Duke" today, it's fast, and I could get away from anyone should the need arises.

Lying in bed, planning my day, my mind wandered to thoughts of Detective Connolly. He is drop-dead gorgeous; the things I would like to do to that man. I shuffled off to the kitchen to make a pot of coffee. The world really can't handle me without my coffee. While it was brewing, I went to the bathroom to take a long hot shower. I could hear the phone ringing in the next room. I listened for the old-school recorder to pick up. It was Connolly's voice. I said to no one in particular, "Did you read my mind, Hot

Connolly." Connolly's voice was asking if I could come down to the station to review his report and sign it. He also said he spoke with the District Attorney, and obviously, there weren't any charges to be filed, as you were the "victim" of an attack and were defending yourself. I said, again to no one in particular, "Thank God! What a pain in the ass that would have been."

I finished with my shower, grabbed my coffee, went to the basement to print Mrs. Nut Farm Dentist's invoice, and returned Hunky Connolly's call. After Granny left the house to me, I renovated the basement. The three floors above ground were in perfect order. Granny was old but very hip. She hired R. Ward, the famous (at least locally renowned) interior designer, to remodel/decorate the three upper floors right before she passed.

Granny thought of everything, including choosing a color palette I would have preferred if I had hired the interior designer myself. After Granny died, I found a note in the freezer beside my favorite ice cream. It said, "I was able to find an interior designer who wasn't afraid to use your favorite colors, but I have no idea how you would like your workshop in the basement. You always loved those damn guns Poppy gave you. You're on your own with the basement." She said, "Use cash with the contractors. They will cut you a deal when you use cash. Love Granny P.S. Poppy taught me that," with a tiny heart and a happy face. Next to the note was a butt load of money, five hundred grand with a sticky note that said, "shhh! Don't tell the lawyers they will put it in probate. You'll have to pay death taxes, and I already paid taxes on this money." she signed with another little heart. I sat on the kitchen floor eating my rocky road and mint chip ice cream, bawling like a baby.

I did most of the work on the basement myself, only hiring contractors to do the specialty work, like electrical and security windows and exterior doors. The original exterior basement door was a large double barn door used in the olden days to bring in the coal for the old coal furnace. The doors were the very last thing I did. The wide opening made it easier to get building materials in the basement. The basement was the entire footprint of the giant Victorian that rested on it above ground. It was a vast blank canvas before I started. Granny replaced the mechanical equipment and tucked it in the back corner of a mechanical room. Next to the mechanical room was a huge bathroom/spa. Granny had the room finished from top to bottom with beautiful neutral-tone marble. The only thing I needed to do was add my toiletries. The basement walls and ceiling were insulated, drywalled, textured, and painted a beautiful dove grey, like I said, a vast blank canvas.

At the front of the basement, the egress windows face east to south/east. I love the light that streams through in the morning, but with the sidewalk about twelve feet away, I wanted more privacy, and security was a must. I didn't want those ugly security bars most people use for added security. I started the long, tedious research and found a company specializing in high-end windows, custom-made to fit any home style. The security windows are shatterproof, break-in proof, and bonus points bulletproof. I spent some serious dough on the security windows and new exterior doors. In all, I spent sixty grand of Granny's freezer money.

Granny was right; it would have been closer to eighty thousand if it wasn't cash. To allow sunlight to filter in but not the prying eyes of strangers from the sidewalk. I went to every antique store and bought every stained-glass window I could find. I had each stained-glass window cut and reframed to fit exactly the interior of the windowsill of each window in the basement.

The floors were bare concrete, I liked the simplistic look, but it just needed to be dressed up a bit. I applied a black, medium gray, and light gray stain over the entire space in a random pattern, giving it a marble appearance, then I applied two coats of high gloss sealer. I loved the wide-open space and wanted to keep it that way. I just wanted to use area rugs and furniture to delineate the workspace.

I had to build a few interior walls for my vault, which had the perfect placement. The front right side of the basement doesn't have any windows, and it's the ideal space to build the vault. I installed high-end garage cabinets with floor-to-ceiling doors along the same wall closer to the back of the house. The cabinet doors open to reveal a workbench with an ammunition reloading press, a precision powder scale, and a die set.

Along the left side of the basement, I built a small Irish-style pub under a couple of windows to give homage to my heritage. I stocked the bar with the best Irish whiskey and craft beers from across the country. When an investigation turns sideways or after a long day and beer doesn't cut it, I can retreat to the bat cave for a tumbler of Knappogue.

My desk sits on a large Jacare silk rug in the front, left corner under the stained-glass windows, with beautiful shafts of light of kaleidoscope colors in the morning sun.

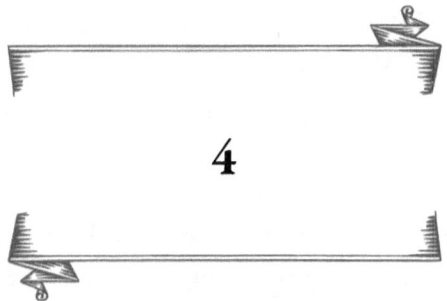

4

AFTER INVOICING MRS. Nut Job Dentist, I returned Sex Pot Connolly's call. I agreed to stop by his office at Sacramento Police Department, a few blocks away. I went into the vault to collect the compact Kimber 45 Caliber 1911 and tucked it in a boot holster in my left boot. I put the full-sized version of 1911, in 45 cal, in the concealed pocket under my right arm. I always carry my weapon under my right arm instead of a holster on my hip when I ride. The bulk of the holster is uncomfortable with my riding gear and doesn't conceal. I'm left-handed, which is convenient to control the throttle and discharge my weapon simultaneously, should an incident occur while riding. Yesterday's scenario I thought would never transpire, but after last night, anything is possible.

I headed towards the carriage house to retrieve "Duke," pausing at the back door of the mud room before taking the flight of stairs; it appeared the coast was clear. I wore black riding pants armored with Kevlar and a black mesh riding jacket. I had my hair tied in a bun at the nape of my neck, hoping no one would recognize me with my blacked-out Arai helmet. Maybe I'll get lucky and will go unnoticed by the bad guys.

Speaking of bad guys, who in the hell are they? After doing some mental Olympics, I shrugged to myself. It could be just about anyone, but the name was Russian, and I recognized it from a few prisoners at FSP. I keep thinking it is due to my time as a CO, but why now? It's been a year since I was shit-canned and several years since I winged the guy with the same last name. Even though my time on the ground was limited, I was in the general population several times. I was mainly assigned to work in the tower.

About a year after I started at Folsom, there was an incident in the yard. A fight broke out between a Russian gang and a Mexican gang. The COs were in the yard trying to break it up. They weren't having much luck. When a Russian was getting ready to shiv one of the COs in the back, I winged the guy with the shiv. The name is the same as "Stanlogovich," but it's a common Russian name. We had three or four in custody with the same last name.

As far as I know, both guys from last night had both hands. It could be related, but it doesn't feel right. Something is missing. I would be pretty pissed off having my hand blown off, but it still doesn't feel right. What was it, what am I missing, and why now?

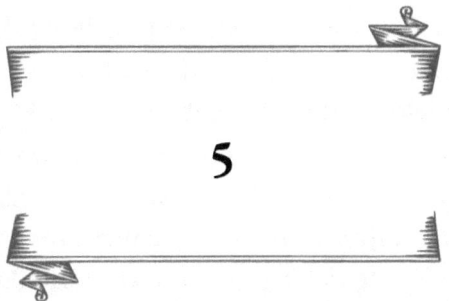

5

DUKE IS A BLACKED-OUT Ducati Panigale V4-S. It's the fastest bike I have ever owned. The 1100 cc engine purrs like a black feline with the capability of reaching 100 mph in five seconds with a top speed of a little under 200 mph. The high-performance "Ohlin's" suspension allows me to electronically adjust it to the dynamic mode on the left handlebar with a quick tap on a screen. I usually tweak my bike's suspension when I take "Duke" out to Sonoma Raceway for open track days, where it rides like it's on rails. Today, I chose "Duke" over the other bikes in the stable in case another SUV driven by crazy Russians shows up again. I can outrun or outmaneuver an SUV or just about anything else with "Duke."

I pulled "Duke" out of the garage into the little courtyard and waited while the garage door went down. I hit the remote to arm the security system in the garage. I turned left out of the gated courtyard onto the L Street alley. I stopped and waited for the gate to roll closed. I typically use the alleys as my very own expressway. Other than an occasional hobo or garbage truck, oops! I mean, residentially challenged or waste management technician, the alleys are empty. I can quickly zip across town. Anyway, at 21st Street, I turned right to head up to H Street, then a left turn took me west to 7th Street, where I took a right, continuing north. Passing the homeless tent city at the old Railyard, heading to the new cop shop on Richards Blvd. I found the parking garage and parked in the visitor section. I left my helmet on until I was inside the station. I announced myself to the desk sergeant, who gave me directions to Sexy Connally's office.

I rapped on the door frame to his open office door. He looked at me from his desk with those big milk chocolate eyes. I think I melted a little or was something else stirring in my jeans? Then he looked at me from head to toe. He had an odd expression on his face as if he were looking at an alien. "So, you ride as well?" he said with a smile, "I ride an old Kawasaki GPZ 650, and I have a Touring Harley as well." I smiled, thinking I liked this guy better every time I talked to him. We talked a little about bikes and what I was riding. He was almost drooling, and I wished he were drooling over me. I told him he could ride "Duke" anytime he wanted.

Then it was all business. Detective Connolly started with Igor Stanlogovich, "His prints were in the system for assault, attempted murder, and a variety of other criminal activities he was involved with." Hot Connolly said the dead Russian guy was associated with some bad guys. I asked him, "Any luck finding the other guy that ran away." He said, "No, they lost the trail almost immediately. There was speculation amongst 'Unies" he had another vehicle stashed in the area." Then I asked him, "When will I get my weapon back." he said, "It will take a couple more weeks to process everything." "Okay, but it's a very special gun. My Poppy gave it to me." Connolly asked, "Did your Poppy hunt elephants with it? That thing is a canon." In a profoundly severe tone, Connolly said, "I spoke directly with the District Attorney, and he agreed with my findings. There will not be any charges filed against you." "Thank you, and I appreciate everything you have done." After signing the statement, he gave me a copy. I stood to go, and he asked if it was okay to walk me out. I was thinking, is it alright if I jump you right here and now? Instead, I smiled and said, "Of course, that would be great." We didn't say much on the way down to the garage, but once the elevator doors opened and we stepped off, he asked, "Could we have lunch or drinks or something." Cool as a cucumber, Connolly seemed a little nervous. I said, "Yeah but suggested eating in, I asked if he had all his vaccinations, and I could attempt to cook dinner." He laughed and said, "He was current on all his shots." This guy was making me all gooey. I offered to cook.

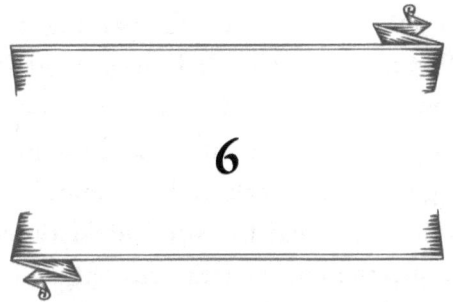

6

I PULLED OUT OF THE PD parking garage, took Richard's Blvd to I-5, and headed south to the Pocket area. My spidey senses went off again, like a radar detector, ding, ding, ding. I glanced in the mirror and caught sight of an all-black, big bus-sized black SUV. I couldn't see who was driving. I think they had the windshield tinted. I wasn't about to go into the Pocket area with only one way in and one way out with a tail. Crazy or not, Mrs. Dentist didn't need this kind of trouble in her life. She's already married to the most boring man on Earth and maybe even on mars.

I leisurely took the I-5 offramp at Florin Road. At the top of the offramp, I took a left turn, crossing over the interstate. I drove the speed limit and didn't change lanes. They appeared to be having a difficult time hanging back. I didn't want them to know I was onto them, so I avoided looking in my mirrors, and at each turn, I used my signal indicator. I was having fun with the cat and mouse game. I took them on a tour of William Land Park, passing through the zoo. Then I parked at the Starbucks, located kitty-corner to Sacramento City College. I walked in wearing my helmet, making a big show standing in line with my back to the front window. I bought a bottle of water; I dropped it in my lightweight backpack I got from the Revzilla's booth at the last open track day. They took the bait and parked the bus on the little residential street next to the Bucks. I took the hallway to the bathrooms and saw the bus parked at the curb. I hoped to see the license plate but couldn't see the plate or the passengers. They definitely had the windshield tinted, so I couldn't tell how many people I was dealing with either. I stood there in the dim hallway light, contemplating my next move. The passenger door opened. Okay, now I know at least two people are in the bus. I said to myself, fine, it's time for the cat to eat the mouse or maybe mice. I walked out to "Duke," taking my time putting on my riding gloves to give them plenty of time to notice I was getting ready to roll. I could see the door shut and the slight movement of the bus as the engine turned over.

Interestingly, all vehicles manufactured or sold in the United States after February 2011 must-have "Daytime Running Lights." The bus-size SUV is at least a 2018 or later GMC-Yukon. Which indicates someone has disabled the DRLs. Alright, boys, let's see who the hell you are, or shall I say, confirm who I think you are. I pulled out of the parking lot onto the little side street, crossing the road to the stop sign. I waited at the stop sign for a nice big gap in the traffic. The bus didn't immediately move. As I took my hand off the brake lever, the wheels on the bus turned to the left. Look who is learning some patience. I slowly rolled off the stop behind the traffic. It was perfect timing. There weren't any cars coming. They had to either follow in behind me without cars separating us or wait for vehicles to hide behind and take a chance of losing me. As luck has it, they followed in behind me. Heading south on Freeport Blvd, I rode at an unbearably slow speed. "Duke" was built for speed, and we didn't like the slow pace all that much, but necessary to gain distance between the pack of cars ahead and me.

Hang on, boys, for a ride. It's time to turn up the heat. At the next traffic light, we caught up to a couple of cars waiting at the red light. I split the lanes to the front of the vehicles. Coming up is the municipal airport about a mile south. There is a slight bend in the road. On the green light, I twisted the grip, but not so much for them to lose sight of me or for me to lose sight of them. I wanted them to continue following me, then right before the bend in the road, I twisted the grip hard this time and shot like a bullet, leaning hard into the turn. Just past the curve in the street, out of sight, there is a frontage road separated from Freeport Blvd with tall, thick pink and white Oleander bushes. By the time I took the frontage road, I was traveling at about 90 mph. At the other end of the frontage road, there is an exit to get back onto Freeport Blvd. I rode down to the end of the frontage road and waited behind the Oleanders. A black flash went by, and I fell behind them, staying about five car lengths back at about 80 mph.

It looks like someone caught on and slammed on their brakes. Windows remained up, so I rolled up next to them, looking at the plate. I stopped "Duke" next to the tinted driver-side window. I gave them a little middle finger wave, indicating they were number one in my book. I popped a wheelie and left them in the middle of Freeport Blvd. A minute later, I backed off the throttle. When I got to where Freeport Blvd turns into the River Levee Road, "Duke" was humming at the speed limit. I continued down the River Levee Road to the first bridge to cross the Sacramento River to head north, back towards Sacramento. I confirmed my suspicions, but at the same time, I was perplexed. California Exempt license plate. Why is an unmarked LEO tailing me, and from what agency?

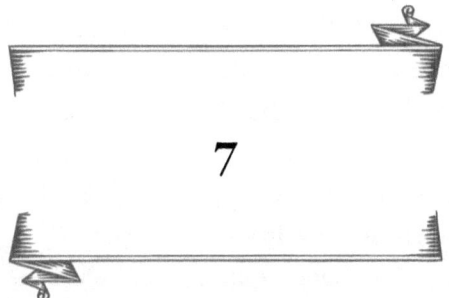

7

CRUISING UP THE RIVER Levee Road on the west bank of the Sacramento River, I decided not to meet with Mrs. Crazy Train Dentist. I didn't want to put her in danger inadvertently. As I rode, I replayed the events over the last few days. And how on two separate occasions, I was located and tailed. I had to reevaluate my security.

"Security" it's a relative statement. My team with USAF Security Forces was responsible for all types of security. Our assignments ranged from securing airfields, defending missile installations, counterterrorism, running convoys, and dignitary security. During "Operation Desert Safe Side," when we invaded Iraq, our orders were Kill or Capture.

As a Private Investigator, I use the education, training, and experience I gained not only for my security but as tools for marks or subjects of an investigation. The tools I use to locate marks or to get to know their habits are the same tools I avoid for my security.

Smartphones are incredibly convenient; they are minicomputers you can carry in your back pocket. You can make calls. You can text. You can send and receive emails. Hell, you can surf the web, but it can also use to track your whereabouts.

People store all kinds of information on their smartphones, from grocery lists to credit cards. There are even apps to store the passwords for their credit cards. Or, if it suits your fancy, you can even pay your bills with an app on your smartphone.

People share almost every aspect of their lives on the internet. People share their likes, dislikes, emotions, and what they are eating, including pictures of what they are eating and where they are eating, adding a real-time pin drop that shows their precise location. They share their entire lives on social media. And if that isn't enough, search engines like Google track your location, what you are looking at on the web, and what you purchase. Don't get me started on Siri or Alexa. The listening device people unwittingly purchased to be lazy. People! Get off your ass and turn the freakin lights on yourself. No wonder we are the fattest nation in the world, for fuck's sake.

Speaking of Alexa, Amazon's brainchild, God forbid you should visit Amazon's site for a particular product because they will inundate you with notifications of similar products. All in the name of convenience. You can't trust technology!

Social media outlets like Facebook, Twitter, and Instagram are some of the tools in my toolbox. With Facebook, your account can be private, but all it takes is a "friend" to set their settings to open, and people can get a glimpse of your activity. These are tools for Private Investigators to learn more about their marks. All of this is why I carry a burner flip phone with prepaid minutes, all purchased with cash.

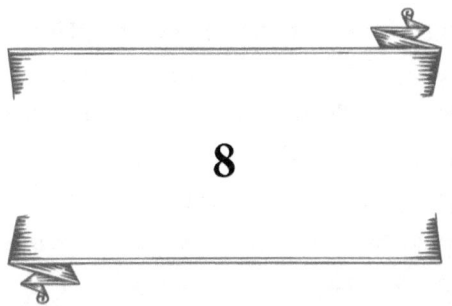

8

WHEN I RIDE, MY SENSES elevate. Riding allows my brain to process what has taken place and to connect the dots. I allow my brain to rant and randomly ramble mentally. Much like hitting the replay button on your T.V. remote repeatedly. Like a movie on a loop. It helps me figure out what the hell is going on. And I can rule out any issues with my security.

The River Cats minor league were in town, so I went to Raley Park to take in a game to clear my head. I hid "Duke" in plain sight, parking it among the twenty other bikes in the parking lot.

The city of West Sacramento contracted Poppy's construction company to build a baseball stadium called Raley Park. It was the last project Poppy completed before he died. Poppy, Granny, and I were gifted a lifetime pass to the River Cats at the home games on opening day.

Walking up to the gate, I got my pass out and put the lanyard around my neck. Once inside the entrance, I went to the bank of lockers to offload my backpack and helmet. I walked up the two flights of stairs to the covered patio of the Governor's Lounge. The baseball field was to the north, and the parking lot to the south. I parked my ass on a barstool where I could see the infield to my left and the parking lot to my right, overlooking where I parked "Duke."

As hot as it was, I left my mesh jacket on to hide the bulge of the 45 under my right arm. I took my low-tech flip phone out of my pocket and sat it on the bar, waiting to turn it on until I ordered my beer. I was in the mood for a dark rich, heavy beer. "Deschutes, Double Chocolate Stout Porter," I said to the bartender. The bartender delivered my beer. I took a big, long pull from it. I picked up the flip phone, turned it on, and called my house to check the messages on my old school recorder.

I went through the prompts to communicate with the voice machine. The electronic voice said, "You have one message, enter a PIN to listen to your message." I listened to the message, then the electronic voice said, "Press one to save the message, and press nine to delete the message." I pressed nine and called Sweetcakes Connolly. When I called him back, he abruptly asked, "What are you up to?" I told him, "I had a rough morning, so I'm sitting at a bar having a beer." In the same snappy tone, he asked, "Where are you?" I told him where I was. He said, "Be there in five," and hung up. Next up, I had to call Mrs. Nutty's Dentist. When she answered my call, I said, "I'm sorry, something came up. I can't make it to see you in person, but I will email you the report and the time-stamped video of the entire surveillance. Your retainer was sufficient payment for my time." She started to debate about it. Cutting her off, I said, "The retainer covered my time, take whatever you think you still owe me, go buy a sexy dress and a bottle of wine and fuck your husband's brains out." Hanging up the phone, turning it off, and dropping it back into my jacket pocket.

I had just finished my first beer when Connolly walked up the top step of the Governor's Lounge. "You look like you had a bad day. Are you still on duty, or can you have a beer?" He said, "I'm off and in serious need of a beer." We both ordered a beer. I told him, "So, what's up?" He asked, "How was your day?" He already seemed to know how my day went. "Why don't you tell me." He said, "I had an interesting visit from the FBI today. Evidently, you shot a person of interest to the FBI. Also, they seem to think you're a little paranoid." I angrily laughed. "That tends to happen when two black SUVs follow you in two days. One of which wanted to kill you and was successful in turning your work car into Swiss cheese. Tell me why the FBI was following me today." Connolly said, "I haven't figured that part out yet, but I think they were expecting someone to make another move on you and wanted to catch them in the middle of it."

"Good to know they think of me as bait," I snarked. Connolly flashed that big, beautiful smile, "They were a little grumpy about losing you today but said you know how to do a nice wheelie." "Well, if they were more forthcoming about their objective, I wouldn't have messed with them so much. Besides, I didn't know who they were until I could get a look at their plate, and not even then I just knew it was a governmental vehicle. If they want to be undercover, they should get rid of the California Exempt plate. All this doesn't seem so urgent for you to come all the way over here to see me. So, spit it out. What was so urgent? What haven't you told me?" "Well, I had some time on my hands this morning and did some checking around, and there's an open bounty on you, and it's pretty high. It's not just the Russians. It's anyone and everyone in the field to take people out." He said with some concern. I said, "Oh! Is that all? Did you happen to find out why there's a contract on me?" Connolly shook his head. "No! But I'm worried."

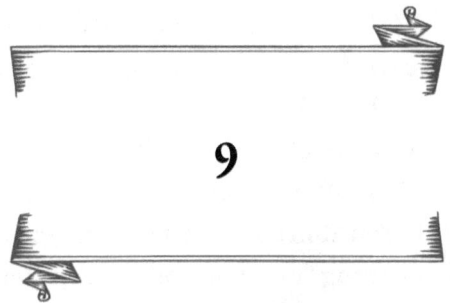

9

HOW DO YOU THINK THE FBI found me this morning?" He said there was a flag associated with the Russian's name. When I put it into the system, they figured whoever it was would eventually show up at the department." Connolly continued to say, "You know, you're pretty careful. You don't have a big internet footprint. I didn't find anything on you today. You don't have a Facebook account, and you don't have Twitter or Instagram. Hell, the website for your business only has a single encrypted email, no office address, no business phone number, and no cellular number." Picking up his phone, I said, "This right here. This smartphone makes it easy for people like me to locate you." Pulling my phone out of my pocket and holding it up, showing him my low-tech flip phone.

"I keep it turned off, and I only use prepaid minutes. It's nearly impossible for anyone to use it to locate me." He asked, "What about your bike? Doesn't it have a GPS tracker on it?" "Nope, I disabled it." "What if someone steals your bike?" "I turn in the insurance claim to my insurance broker, and I buy another one. I rather do that than for someone to have the capability of tracking me." Connolly said, "Okay, maybe this won't be as bad as I thought it would be."

Sipping his beer, He asked, "Who's winning the game?" "Honestly, I have no clue. I haven't even been watching. I've been watching Duke" "Duke?" I said, "My bike, it's down there in the pack of bikes." "Awe! hiding in plain sight." "Yup, I knew I could watch it from right at this spot." "You come here often, do ya?" "Yeah, I have a season pass." He smiled his big sexy smile. "I have a season pass too." He downed the rest of his beer. "How about that dinner, you up for company?" I stammered, "Um, yes, yes, I am, but we will have to order takeout. The only thing I have in the house is ice cream."

Connolly followed me out of the ballpark. We crossed the golden "Tower Bridge" with the view of the State Capital straight ahead. I took Connolly through downtown, making several left turns and right turns, went through Midtown, kept going to East Sacramento, and circled back to my alley expressway. A couple of houses down from my back gate, I spotted the FBI rig and was completely good with them being there. I hit the eight-foot security gate remote, which started rolling open to one side. Then click another button on the remote for the garage. I motioned for Connolly to park his car in the open carport bay. He did the cop thing and backed into the carport. With the gate closed and "Duke" tucked away in the garage, we headed to the back door leading to the mud room. The low beep, beep, beep reminded me to punch in my code to disarm the security system, 766443. Then I hit a button that said occupied. Connolly stood perfectly still in one place as I went through the motions. I said, "The exterior is alarmed, but the interior motion sensors are off." "So, it's safe to move about without getting laser beamed," he said with a shit-eating grin. Then his eyes dilated, turning from milk chocolate to almost black, and in a deep low voice, said, "You have the prettiest green eyes," bent down and kissed me a soft, sweet kiss. Then turned on his heels, asking, "You have any beer in this joint?' "Um yeah!" stuttering my words a bit. I caught my breath and grabbed a couple of beers. "So, what sounds good to eat." His eyes darkened again, looking at me like I was on the menu. I felt a flash of heat wash over me. Then the shit-eating grin was on his gorgeous face again. He knew exactly what he was doing and was having fun tormenting me. "How about pizza? I'll order an extra one for the FBI rig out back." "You better get one for the rig out front, too, or they'll get their little feelings hurt again." I peeked out the front. There was another black bus out there. "I hope they aren't announcing their twenty over the air with my name attached to it." Connolly got a grim expression on his face and said, "Shit!" He dug out his billfold and pulled out a business card. "Can I use your low-tech flip phone?" I handed it to him. He turned it on and dialed the number from the business card. "Hello, Agent Baxter, This is Detective Connolly from Sacramento Police Department. I have a question brought up to me by Miss Foxx. Are you and your team on radio silence while sitting at her house?" He listened intently to Agent Baxter's response. "Okay, have you used Miss Foxx's name while on the radio?" I can hear what sounded like Charlie Brown's teacher talking, "Wah, Wah, Wah" "Fuck! You are fucking morons. You better hope to God there isn't anyone in the area with a scanner. You tell your fucking team radio silence; you think you can handle that?" I exclaimed, "Well, they blew any chance of getting pizza from me. Come with me; we better get ready." We walked down the stairs to the bat cave. I slid the giant red barn-style doors to each side, revealing the thick steel door. I punched in another code,

5750, to open the vault. We walked in; I began shopping for defense weapons.

I shut the vault after picking out a couple of semi-automatic handguns and a couple of shotguns. The alarm on the vault automatically notifies me with a little beep, beep, beep when it's armed. Then I went to my desk, turned on the desktop computer, and initiated a complete perimeter camera surveillance with alarms. Connolly asked, "What the hell did you do?" I explained, "I was a USAF Security Force Sniper; I specialized in security. I have the perimeter cameras armed at twelve feet. If anyone comes onto this property, we will get notified of the breach with an internal bell. Each zone with a different sounding alarm."

After handing Connolly one of the shotguns, I said, "Let's find something to eat in the kitchen. I'm starving." I turned to go upstairs. Connolly gently grabbed my arm, spun me around to face him, took my face in his enormous hands, and kissed me long and deep.

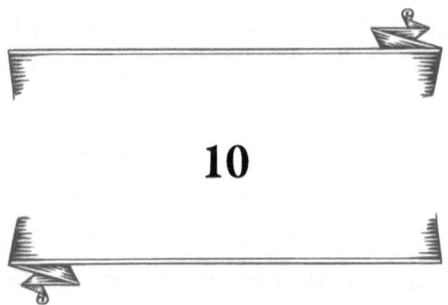

10

"WOW! THAT WAS SOME kiss," I said As I tried to get my composure to answer the landline. "Hello, it's for you." Handing the phone to Connolly. Connolly asked, "Did you run the plate?" He listened for a minute. Then he said, "Ok, we're locked and loaded in here. We'll keep an eye out. Thanks for the call." Connolly hung up the phone and said, "It was the super-smart FBI agent, Baxter. They spotted a car doing a grid search and ran the plate, but the license plate doesn't match the vehicle description." I asked, "Can you call it in, put a "BOLO' on it? Maybe a patrol unit will locate them.

Whoever it is, is trying to locate the team from the radio chatter. If the FBI team remains radio silent, he won't find us. Besides, this house is in my Granny's maiden name, and all my vehicles are in the same family trust name. Your cruiser isn't visible from anywhere outside of the property. They can't get in the courtyard without us knowing about it." Connolly called dispatch and had a cruiser patrol the area for the vehicle with the stolen plates.

"Ok, let's go make something to eat. I'm starving." We went upstairs to the kitchen and found some Keto fettuccine; I got a big pot to start the water. I have some sweet basil in the freezer. Connolly looked in the freezer and said, "The only thing I see here is two gallons of rocky road and mint chip ice cream." I said, "It's in the door next to the beer mugs." I drained the pasta and tossed it with grass-fed butter from my ancestors' homeland and a little olive oil. I added the sweet basil and a hand full of sundried tomatoes. We stood at the counter, chowing down on the pasta. Our handguns were next to each of our plates.

Connolly said with a mouth full of pasta, "Thought you couldn't cook. The pasta is amazing, so simple, yet absolutely gourmet." "That's what I like, a simple man." We topped dinner off with another beer.

Then a polite little bell chimed. I said, "That's the alarm for the back gate." The floodlight came on simultaneously as the bell chimed. We peeked out at the kitchen window; we saw a shadowy figure run in the opposite direction of the FBI bus. I told Connolly, "Let's go see who it was. Follow me." He said, "With pleasure," following me to the living room. I flopped down on the large, overstuffed sofa; I patted the seat next to me for Connolly to park it next to me on the sofa. Connolly sat down. We both put our feet on the coffee table, and I switched on the TV.

I went to the menu button, scrolling to DVR. A wiry black man appeared on the screen. I said, "It's okay. It's just Sam. I know him. He's a friend from my team. He has PTSD and prefers living outdoors." Connolly asked, "Is that another PC term, homeless?" I said, "He's different. It's more like camping. He doesn't like the confinement of the traditional sticks and bricks house." Connolly asked, "Does he usually show up at night?" I shook my head, "No! Now that you mention it, he has never shown up after dark. I wonder what that's all about?" "Well, if we get through the night, we can look for him in the morning and check on him." I said, "We will get through the night. No one can get in here." Connolly said, "You remember how your car looked? there's a lot of windows in this house." I said, "As long as the idiots outside keep the radio silence, they won't find this house, and even if they do, every window in the house is bulletproof. So, let's go to bed." He smiled his gorgeous smile and said, "Lead the way." We climbed the stairs to the second floor. I walked through the bedroom to the bathroom and turned on the light, letting it filter into the bedroom. We met in the middle of the room, undressing each other, clothes falling to the floor. Kissing each other, I whispered. "Follow me." He said, "Again, with pleasure!" I led him to the bathroom.

I turned on the shower, with shower heads from all directions beating on our skin. Connolly's body was hard with long, strong muscles. He kissed me on the neck, kissing me on my hardened nipples, he kissed me on my belly, heading south, he kissed me on my, ohhh my! I took him in my mouth. He moaned a low guttural sound. He picked me up and carried me to the bed. He continued to kiss me in all the good places as I was about to. He crawled up my body, kissing me, and slowly, rhythmically inserted himself inside me. I almost instantly exploded, but I wanted to wait for Connolly. We exploded with each other, lying there wholly, completely spent, and we fell fast asleep.

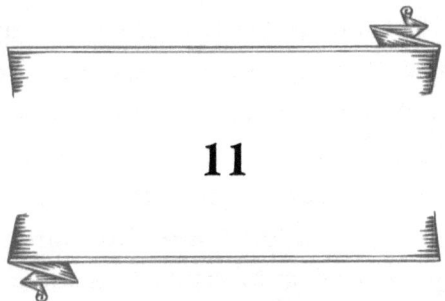

11

WE WOKE TO A BRIGHT light streaming in around the heavy curtains. The light seemed manufactured. I could hear, chuf, chuf, chuf. I got up to see what the hell was going on; it was a Sacramento Police Department helicopter hovering over a building across the street. An intense spotlight was shown on the house. Connolly said, "What the fuck is going on?" as he reached for the phone to call dispatch. He listened to the person on the other end of the line. "Okay, call me at this number and keep me posted but do not. I repeat, do not use any names for who lives at this residence." Connolly hung up the phone and said, "It was the vehicle with the stolen plates. Patrol found it, pulled it over, and the guy started shooting at the officer when he approached the vehicle." I asked, "The officer, okay?" He said, "Yes, the asshole missed him. He took off running, the officer called for backup, and the whole damn department showed up." I said, "So it has nothing to do with us at this very moment." I took him in my hand, and he immediately saluted. Round two was even more intense, with exploratory kissing and caressing. I rolled off Connolly, soaked with sweat and sex. I asked, "If he wanted to join me with a shower?" but he didn't move until the following day when he smelled the coffee.

I handed him a cup when he walked into the kitchen. He kissed me long and deep. He made my toes curl, and I melted into him and sighed. "Knock it off. We need to find Sam." He said, "This coffee is amazing. What the hell is in it? I've never tasted anything like it." I smiled and winked, "I guess you will need to come around more often to get a cup," and walked out of the kitchen to shower. Connolly joined me in the shower to conduct an exploratory investigation. I don't think a regular shower will ever be the same from here on out. Connolly watched my ritual of jasmine body oil, then lotion. I prefer as little underwear as possible, so commando on the bottom and stick on a bra on top. I dressed in a pair of jeans with designer holes in the knees and a scoop-neck tank top.

I said, "I'll be right back; your clothes should be done by now." He said, "Clothes?" I said, "I steam-cleaned your suit and washed your shirt and underwear. I didn't think you wanted to put on yesterday's underwear." He said, "I wasn't going to, but thanks." I raised my eyebrow and said, "Yum commando." He said, "I can say the same thing." Tossing his towel at me as I was walking out. I brought his clothes in and watched Connolly as he got dressed. His magnificent strong hard body flexed and twitched with each movement. I was, creaming my jeans. I thought, what is wrong with you, Foxx? Get it together. Connolly said, "If it's okay with you, I'll drive my car. No one would think to tail a cop car looking for you." I said," Sure, I don't care what we drive." I set the alarm system, and we went out of the gate. Connolly stopped to wait for the security gate to close before driving off. We took a right towards East Sacramento, in the direction of Sam's camp on the bank of the American River near CSUS.

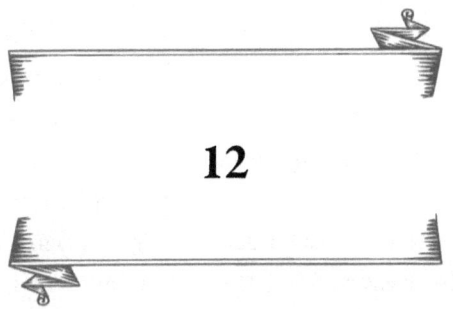

12

CONNOLLY AND I TOOK J Street to East Sacramento. We parked at St. Francis Catholic High school on Elvas Avenue. We jay-walked across Elvas Avenue through the CSUS Hornets stadium parking lot to the American River trail. Students use the trail on top of the American River levee. They use it to travel back and forth from the athletic fields on the west side of the American River and to the main campus on the east side of the river. Below the trail, homeless camps are scattered along the river bank. Connolly followed me on a dirt trail leading to Sam's tent. Most of the homeless camps have trash or junk they have collected from dumpster diving spewed all over their camp. Sam is different. He is squared away. He keeps his camp clean; he takes advantage of the shelter's free showers and washes his clothes at the laundromat. I called out to the tent. Sam, it's Roxxy. Are you home? Hello, anyone home? A small, shy voice behind the bushes said, "Sam isn't home. He didn't come home last night." I said, "Who's there, Maggie? Is that you?" A young twenty-something girl stepped out and said, "Yeah, it's me, Hi Roxxy." I said, "Hi Maggie, how are you; you look a little scared. Is everything alright?" She started to cry and said, "I'm worried about Sam. He always comes home at night. I get scared at night, so he always comes home to ensure I'm okay." I asked Maggie if she knew where he had gone, and she shook her head with tears running down her face. I said, "It will be alright. I will go find Sam and tell him you are worried about him." Without another word, she nodded and stepped back behind the bushes. I walked up the trail with Connolly trailing behind me. Lost in thought. Connolly said, "Roxx, Roxx are you listening?" I turned and said, "Sorry, What?" He repeated himself, "are you okay?" I said, "Umm, I don't know." tears swelled in my eyes. I blinked hard, trying not to cry, but as soon as Connolly saw my eyes, he swallowed me up in his arms, and I lost it. "Sam is my friend; I think he was trying to warn me last night, and now he is missing." Connolly held me tight in his arms as I cried into his chest. He held my face in his hands, softly kissed me, and said, "It will be alright. We will find Sam." A light bulb went off, and I said, "What day is it?" Connolly said, "Saturday, why?" I said, "Come on, grabbing his hand, let's go. I think I know where to find Sam. He once told me whenever he is conflicted. He will go to church. He said he doesn't have just one church he attends. If you attend several, you can always find one with an open door." Connolly said, "I grew up Catholic. Who goes to church on Saturday?" I said, "Jehovah's Witness, there are two Kingdom Halls near here. The one closest to my place is on Del Paso Blvd. The one closest to here is on Hurley Way." We went to the Kingdom Hall on Hurley Way first. We walked into The Kingdom Hall. The meeting had already begun, and we quietly sat in the back, looking around for Sam. "Sam isn't here," I whispered, "let's go." We stood to leave, and the "Elder" speaking to the congregation stopped and said, "Ma'am, is there something we can help you with?" I turned to look. The small congregation turned in their seats to look at us. I said, "I'm sorry. We didn't mean to interrupt your meeting." I looked around the room. Their faces were soft kind faces. I said, "We are looking for my friend Sam. He is missing and may be in danger." Suspiciously, The Elder asked, "And who are you?" I said, "My name is Roxanne Foxx. Sam knows me by Roxxy. And this is Detective Connolly." The Elder said, "We are just about to take a break for coffee and cookies. Can you please wait a moment?" I nodded, and we sat back in our seats. The Elder spoke a couple more minutes, then said to the congregation, "Let's take a small break." The Elder walked back to where Connolly and I were now standing. He said, "Do you mind," He gestured to follow him, and we walked down a small corridor to an office. Sam was lying on a sofa, badly bruised and with a split lip. I sat on the sofa's edge and asked Sam, "Who did this to you?" He said, "A couple of guys in the camp took a job to find you, they knew you and I were friends. I tried to warn you last night, and they jumped me when I was almost home." I didn't tell them where you lived. I told them we only see each other at the Starbucks on Arden and Howe. They didn't believe me until I said you didn't want a homeless dude like me knowing where you lived. They seemed to believe that." "Come on, Sam. I want you to go to the hospital." Sam said, "No, I'm not going to that damn VA hospital. I'll die for sure." I smiled and said, "I can take you to Mercy General." He shook his head, "I can't afford that place." "Sam, I didn't say anything about you paying for it. You saved my life for the second time. The least I can do is get you patched up." He said, "No, it's just bruises and a fat lip. I need to get to the camp to check on Maggie." I said, "We just saw Maggie a little while ago. She seemed scared and worried about you." Sam said, "Yeah, she's just a kid." "If you won't let me take you to a doctor. Let me take you home." He said, "You need to stay away from there. A whole network of homeless assholes has joined in to look for you. They'll do just about anything to get their fix; the contract is ten large dead or alive." I asked, "Did they say who or why there's a contract?" "They said a name. It sounded like it was Ukraine, but I'm not sure." "Sam, this is Detective Connolly. If you need to get ahold of me, call Sac PD and ask for him." Connolly said, "Better yet! here," he dug into his wallet and came up with a card. He said, "Day or night, Sam, and thank you, Sir, for your service." Sam took the card, tried to smile but grimaced in pain, touching his fat lip, and said, "My pleasure, Sir." I hugged Sam and said, "I'm so sorry, Sam. I have no idea what this is all about, but I will get to the bottom of it, I promise." Sam said solemnly, "I know. Roxxy, I know, but you should be careful." The Elder walked us out. I said Thank you to him and shook his hand. I reached into my back pocket and pulled out a couple of hundred-dollar bills. "Will you please give this to Sam? He won't take it from me. Maybe you can suggest he and Maggie get a motel for a couple of days." The Elder said, " I will take him to camp to collect Maggie and some belongings and take him to a clean, inexpensive motel after our meeting." Connolly pulled out another card, handed it to The Elder, and shook his hand. Connolly and I walked out of the Kingdom Hall. I looked up at Connolly, kissed him, and said, "Thank you." He smiled, kissed me on the forehead, and hugged me. I said, "I think it's time to talk to the oh-so-very smart FBI agent but first, let's eat. I'm starving." He chuckled and said, "Only a military member could think of food at a time like this." I said, "I can think of food almost anytime." He said, "Okay, get in. Where to?" I said, "I'm in the mood for fish tacos?" He said, "Swabbies it is." and put the car in gear. I said, "Nope, even better, Elk Horn Saloon across the river." He was indignant and said, "Swabbies have the best fish tacos in Sacramento." I said, "Most people think that until they have Elk Horns."

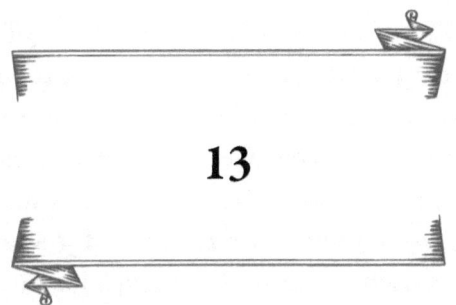

13

CONNOLLY WAS TELLING the owner of Elk Horn Saloon; he converted. Laughing, telling Skittle he thought I was off my rocker when I insisted Elk Horn Saloon had the best fish tacos in town. We said our goodbyes to Skittle. Walking out to Connolly's car, He said, "I hate to admit this, but you were right." "Wait, what did you say? Did you just say I was right?" Connolly smacked me on the ass and said, "You are cruising for it, aren't you? Isn't it enough to be right, and I agree you are right without rubbing it in?" "Well, let's see, Umm, Nope!" Connolly hugged me and gave me a sweet soft kiss. He said, "Alright, let's see the moronic FBI agent." "Okay, but first, maybe we should do a drive-by at my house so I can see the cars parked there." We drove down the street in front of my house and then down the alley. Then along the surrounding blocks. No one is hanging out in their cars, but there is a panel van with tinted windows. I gave the plate to Connolly, and he called it in. He hung up his cell phone and said, "It'll be a couple of minutes." Connolly was scrolling through the recent call list to find the dumbass FBI agent's phone number when his phone rang. He answered with "Connolly speaking. "Oh hey, girl." Talking in a girly ghetto slang speak. "Hangs on, I'm gonna put you on speaker. I got my girl here, Mizz Foxx. She be a Fox if you know what I'm saying." I was looking at Connolly like he went bat-shit crazy as he clicked the speakerphone button on his iPhone. Connolly said, "Ok, girl, we here." The very deep voice on the other end of the line said while smacking gum, "That plate you called about is Homeland." Connolly said, "Girl, get out. Homeland doesn't register vehicles under Homeland." The voice said,

"Hmm don't you think I know that?" With a little attitude. I could picture the voice at the other end, hand on hip with a black girl's head roll with a whole lot of sass. I smiled, listening to their interaction. The voice went on. Smacking gum, saying, "I recognized the address. So, I looked it up and did a google street view. It's a plain glass office door downtown, but the office door right next to it has the Homeland seal on it." "Damn, girl." Connolly said, "That's some fine-ass detective work." The voice said, "Girl, you know it." Then the voice was gone with a click. I slowly turned in my seat, "Who was that? The voice was awfully deep to be a girl." Connolly said, "That's Jose. He is one of my detectives. He is a Mexican male but identifies as a young black girl. I'm the only one he is open with at the department. We have been friends forever. When you meet him, he goes by Juanita." Smiling, I said, "That doesn't seem like a black girl's name." Connolly said, "He's still Mexican even though he identifies with a young black girl." Shrugging. "What can I say? He's complicated." "Well, whatever he identifies as, that was good police work. I think I know, but really? What the hell is Homeland doing sitting on my house? Connolly, can you go back around, please?"

Connolly looked at me sideways. "I don't think that's such a good idea. You kind of look pissed." "Well, that's because I am, and if you don't drive me back around, I'm getting out right here." "Ok!" he sighed. "I'll drive back around." Connolly double-parked, and I got out. I went around to the curbside of the panel van and banged on the door. No answer. I banged again and said, "I know you're in there. Your van just rocked when you moved in there."

The sliding door flew back, and a fat, unshaven man said in a raspy voice through his teeth, "Are you freakin insane?" "What are you doing sitting on my house?" He snarked, "Oh, I don't know. You shot a Russian bad guy; you figure it out." Connolly came around the back of the van and said, "Everyone calm down." The fat guy said, "Tell your girlfriend to calm down." Connolly grabbed the fat guy by the collar, yanked him out of the van, and shoved him against the door. Connolly said in an eerie calm but scary stern voice, "You need to be more respectful to Miss Foxx."

I said, "Look, I don't know what is going on or why. Someone tried to kill me. Then my friend got the crap beat out of him for not telling some asshole homeless guys where I live. Then the idiots in the black SUV almost got my place located by radio chatter, and now Homeland is sitting on my house. There's only so much I can freakin take of this bullshit. Please tell me what you can". The fat guy's shoulders slumped a little, and I knew I got to him. He said, "I get it. It's a bit much to take, the only thing I can say is the guy you shot was on a watch list, and we think we know who the other guy was, but we aren't sure. We hoped he would show up here so we could scoop him up." "Oh, That's great! So, I'm the bait for you guys too. Fucking great!" He said, "We have your house surrounded, including above." I said, "Above?" He pointed up. I whispered, "Satellite." He nodded. I looked at Connolly. "Come on, Connolly, let's go." Jumping in the car. I said, "Let's go. I need to go to my house; hurry, let's go." "Okay, but will you please tell me what the fuck is going on when we get there?" I nodded, "Yes, Please hurry."

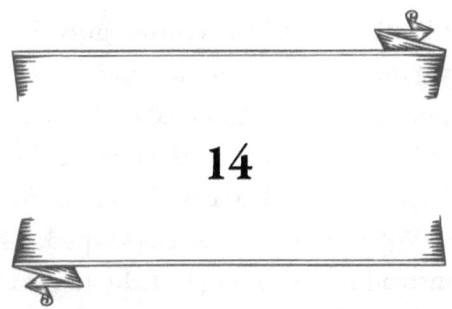

14

CONNOLLY PULLED HIS cruiser into the courtyard. The security gate closed behind us, and he backed the car into the carport. I smiled. "You ready?" "Yes, let's go inside so you can tell me why you freaked when the Homeland guy pointed up." I nodded. We walked into the mud room and punched 766543 into the alarm keypad, which armed the system instead of disarming it. I shouted to the ceiling, "You fucking son of a bitches. you better get your fucking asses over here in less than five minutes, or I'm going to start making calls." I angrily punched in the code again, 766543. The alarm was disabled. Connolly stood quiet, taking it all in, and jumped slightly when the front doorbell rang. I looked at him and said, "That's them." I went to the front door with Connolly following. I opened the giant ornate door wide open and sucker-punched the tall blond. He howled, "Fuck Roxxy, you broke my nose." "You!" I said to the technician, pointing my finger in his face. "Go get them out, every single one. If I find one, and I will find it. No one is as good as I am. I'll come after you. Am I clear, asshole?" He nodded and started working. "Craig, if you put anything in my bedroom or bathroom, I'm going to kick your fucking ass, then I'm going to make my calls, you copy?" Craig nodded. I paused to calm myself down, then I calmly smiled and started to say. Craig said, "Oh no, why are you smiling? I've seen you do that right before almost killing that guy." I put my finger on my lips, "Shhh, shut up, Craig." I listened to the technician's footsteps. "Okay, what is going on? and remember, now I know your team is involved. I will verify what you tell me, so don't bullshit me." "Okay, Roxxy, okay." Craig started rattling, "The guy you killed was on our list." I put my hand up in a stop position. "Our list or a watch list?" Craig continued, "Our list, well, like both lists "Our" list and the watch list." I said, "Okay, who is Igor Stanlogovich? That's the name on his ID. What was his real name?" Craig said, "I know. It's his real name. Like he was thumbing his nose at us." I said, "Okay, I have never heard of that but go on." Craig said, "We are actually looking for his boss, but the boss is smarter and has taken a new identity. He fell off the face of the earth about five years ago." I asked, "What makes you think he is here in Sacramento?" "Because his twin brother was shot in the back of the head by you." "And you thought putting eyes and ears in my house would lead you to him." Craig got nervous again. "It was my new boss. He thought he came after you because you screwed him out of a deal or double-crossed him." "What? What's your boss's name?" Craig's got the defeated slump, "John O'Brien." I said, "One more thing, why is the FBI in on this?' He said, "The boss had an agent killed, the sick bastard deboned him, literally removed his entire skeletal, then mailed the skin of his body in his suit. He looked like his body was deflated. Then they mailed the bones to us after they were boiled clean and put back together. With a note that said, "I have a bone to pick with you." I said, "How did Igor Stanlogovich get demoted to a wheel man to hit a female civilian?" Craig said. "We don't know." The technician walked in and said, "All done." I said, "How many?" "Thirty, ma'am." "Open your case." The kid shuffled from one foot to the other and looked at Craig for help. Craig nodded, and the kid opened his case. I picked one up and smiled, and did a quick count.

I slowly looked up at Craig. "Crap! you idiot, I told you not to try and pull a fast one on her. I told you before we walked in here she would catch you." Then gave him a big Gibbs slap across the back of the head that lifted him off his heels. "Now go get it." He came back. I said, "Let me see it." I held my hand out, palm up. He dropped it in my hand. I looked at it closely, smiled, and handed it back to him. The kid shrugged, dropped it in his case, and walked out the front door. As Craig was about to leave, I said, "I'll be making my call regarding your boss. He may not be in on Monday." He said, "One can only hope. He is a total tool, Roxx." as he walked out the door. I shut the door behind them, locking it. Turning on my heels, I went to the keypad in the mud room. Quietly still watching, Connolly followed me. I hit the function key, punching in the code 071509. We listened to the beeping. It finished then I alarmed the system without the motion sensors. I crooked my finger to Connolly for him to follow me to the basement. At the vault, I slid the big barn doors to each side of the vault door. I punched in the code 5157. It made a musical note that sounded like the music from Wizard of Oz when the witch was riding the bicycle. Which meant they tried to get in here too. Connolly still didn't say anything. He just watched. I punched 051509, beep, beep, beep, then punched 5157. Then the five rods of two-inch steel in the vault door were extracted from the concrete floor. Sitting at my work bench, I opened the drawer, pulled out a small but powerful sat phone, and turned it on. I hit function #69 and put the phone to my ear. I said, "Hello Sir, no, I'm fine. No Sir, I promise I'm okay." Connolly stood off to one side of the room with a calm, serene expression, taking it all in. I said, "I could use your assistance. Well, sir, my old team put eyes and ears in Granny's house." I held the phone away from my ear as he yelled. I said, "Craig tried to tell the new guy John O'Brien not to, but Craig was ordered. So Craig was following orders." I listened for a minute and said, "Thank you, sir. I miss you too. Yes, sir, I will, ok love you too." That got an eyebrow raised and nothing else from Connolly. I disconnected, turned the phone off, and put it back in the drawer. "Well, John O'Brien should pack his bag appropriately for Siberia." Connolly didn't have to ask. I launched right into everything. "That was my Godfather. He reports directly to the President. He isn't the public figure you are thinking of, and his role is top secret. In college, I was a radio geek. I designed and hold the patent to the bugs you saw the technician retrieve. I designed this alarm system too, so if someone used an electronic decoder, it would appear to them to be armed but wouldn't re-arm, so I would know if someone was there. With the combination of the fat guy pointing up at the satellite and the alarm system being unarmed, I knew it was my old team. We were farmed out to Homeland all the time. My team's standing orders are Kill or Capture anyone on our list. The Homeland's list is a watch list. If they are on our list, we get notified if they get a hit on a name. I designed the vault alarm system. If anyone used an electronic decoder, the system would recognize it, and the steel rods won't raise.

My Godfather recruited me; he and my Poppy have been best friends since kindergarten. The team, for all the world, was to be viewed as a "Security Forces Team," but only a few people knew of the team's existence and actual duties. I'll tell you more later. Would you mind staying another night here?" Connolly wrapped his arms around me and said, "I thought you would never ask. I just need to go to my place and get some things."

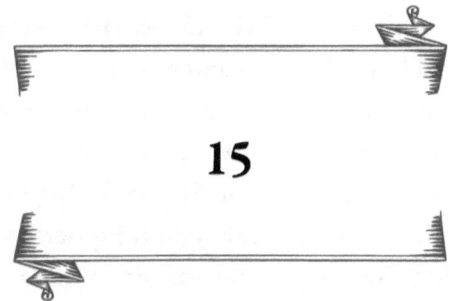

15

I WOKE TO THE SOUND, clink, clink, clink, coming from the third floor. I smiled and went to the bathroom. To scrape the hair off my teeth before heading to the kitchen to make coffee. I made my special coffee concoction in two giant travel mugs sporting the Starbucks logo and headed to the third floor. Clink, clink, clink, I quietly stood at the door watching Connolly lifting massive amounts of weight. One last clink, and he sat up from the bench press. Not an ounce of fat, his body glistening with beads of sweat. His light brown hair darkened at the collar. His athletic build isn't bulky but strong as an ox.

I stood there drooling and said huba, huba. He smiled a shy smile as I handed him his coffee. He said, "This gym is amazing, the mirrors on every wall are a bit much, but the equipment is top-notch. How the hell did you get this equipment up here?" "I can't take credit for any of it, my Granny hired an interior decorator before she passed, and this was part of the remodeling. The mirrors, well, you know they are everywhere, but if I don't watch my form, it will go in the toilet. So happy accident."

He nodded to two long white units over each window and said, "What are those?" I laughed and said, "Those almost got the most sought-after interior designer fired in the middle of the job." He smiled and said, "Do tell!"

"Well, Granny had her mind set on those things, they are air conditioning units, and the designer said they were too ugly and tried to refuse to install them." Laughing, I said, "Ward didn't have a chance. Granny thought I would get too hot working out up here, and she wasn't going to have it. She told Ward that if she weren't creative enough to blend the a/c units in with the wall coloring, she would sever ties and hire someone capable of the job." He smiled and said, "Granny was right. It's hotter than a Mexican lunch up here." I flipped the switch next to the door, and the a/c units started humming with cool air. Connolly said, "I would have loved to meet Granny. She sounds like a hoot." "She would have loved you. If you want to steam or a sauna, it's through there." Nodding at the center mirrored panel.

He said, "Oh, I see. Even the little handles are mirrored." He walked over and pulled on the handle; the mirrored door swung open to expose a short hallway with a hot sauna lined with fragrant cedar planks on one side of the hallway. The combo steam/shower room on the other. His thick beautiful lips turned into a wicked little smile as he crooked his finger at me. I followed him into the hallway, where he untied the belt of my robe and pulled it off each shoulder with a little kiss. As it dropped to the floor, standing there naked, he kissed each of my nipples.

I muttered, "One of us is overdressed." I pulled his gym shorts down. While I was in the vicinity, I took him in my mouth. He quietly moaned, tangling his fingers in my already "just fucked" looking hair. As I stood, kissing my way up his salty washboard abs, moving up to his magnificent pecks, then to his thick kissable lips. He opened the steam room door; I stepped in, and he pressed himself up against my ass, reaching around me to find out how wet I was. He slid his finger farther between my legs. He bent me over and inserted himself while still reaching around my body, caressing me as I exploded. He followed my lead with a more intense explosion. He gently moved my hair and kissed the back of my neck. I switched the settings from steam to rain shower. We gently and purposefully washed each other.

We kissed long, deep gentle kisses, and we made love. Looking into each other's eyes, we simultaneously came for a second time. We lay on the tile while the shower beat on Connolly's back. In the distance, I can hear a low ring. It was Connolly's phone ringing one flight down on the nightstand in my bedroom. He moaned, rolling over onto his back, the shower now hitting my belly. He stood up, then helped me to my feet. With a quick kiss, he stepped out of the shower. His Cell phone stopped ringing, then immediately started again. Damn! as he grabbed a towel and handed it to me and then one for himself. He wrapped the towel around his waist just below the light brown love trail. I followed him to my bedroom and into the dressing room. I started looking for clothes to wear.

The cell phone stopped ringing and immediately started up again. Connolly snatched the cell phone off the nightstand and barked, "Hello!" He listened for several minutes and asked, "Is this credible information? Whose informant is he?" After listening for a moment, he asked. "How is Johnson's relationship with him?" He listened for several more minutes, then said, "Okay, thanks, oh text me Johnson's number, please. Alright, copy!" As soon as he hung up, his phone dinged with Johnson's cell phone number. He tapped the number on the screen, and it dialed Johnson.

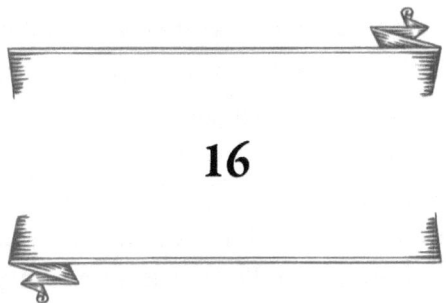

16

CONNOLLY SAID, "HEY Brother, what you got?" He sat down on the side of the bed and listened intently. He said, "And you believe this informant? Uh-huh, yeah, ok, yeah, ok, Thanks, Brother, I owe you one." I popped my head out of the dressing room and said, "What's up?" As Connolly was about to answer, the intercom at the courtyard gate at the alley chimed. "Hold that thought." I pushed the intercom button on the intricate phone system on my night table. "Hello?" A frantic voice was yelling over the intercom, "It's me, Sam." Sam yelled, "They took her, Roxxy. I need your help." frantically yelling and sobbing, "Please help me, Roxxy, they took her." I said, "I'm coming down. Hang tight, Sam." I looked over at Connolly. He was dressed and ready to roll. I grabbed my compact 45 Cal from the nightstand drawer and slipped it into my back pocket. We were taking the stairs two at a time; Connolly relayed Johnson's intel from his informant in his professional cop radio voice, clear, precise, and rapid-fire. Dan Aykroyd popped into my head. "Just the facts, ma'am!" Did I mention I'm a little bent? As we reached the main floor, he continued, "Johnson's unit handles the department's homeless outreach program, helping those who want help and want to help themselves.

He was, additionally, handling the person-on-person crimes in the homeless community. Johnson has done a phenomenal job and built a relationship with those he has helped over the years. His informant witnessed an attack on a black male and the abduction of a young white female." I said, "Sam and Maggie!" I snatched my keys as I passed through the mudroom, then sown the backdoor stairs to the courtyard.

Sam was standing at the gate with his head pressed to the rod iron bars, bloody and bruised. He looked like a caged animal. I started to click the button for the gate on my key fob. Connolly touched my hand, looking me in the eyes. His milk chocolate eyes turned to an intense dark coffee brown. "Let me take a look down the alley, stay out of sight for a second." I nodded but wanted to rush the gate to Sam. He looked horrified. A sight I wasn't used to seeing. I fought side by side with Sam. He is one of the bravest warriors I have ever seen. Connolly looked up and down the alley and said, "All clear, good to go." I stepped in full view of the gate, hitting the button on the fob. As the gate opened, Sam collapsed in our arms. We pulled him inside the gate and closed the gate. We dragged him around the front of the carriage house in the courtyard. "Sam! Sam!" I shouted. I checked for a pulse, "He's alive, but his pulse is very weak." Just as I was saying, "We need to get him to a hospital." Sam opened his eyes and grasped my hand. "You have to save her. She's my baby girl." Sam was unconscious and barely alive. Connolly tossed me the keys to his cruiser, "Open the doors." He yanked Sam up and threw him over his shoulder in one fell swoop, like a sack of potatoes. I ran ahead and opened the doors, and got behind the wheel. Hitting the gate fob and the accelerator simultaneously, I reached the gate's opening as it opened with just an inch to spare. I hit the fob again just as I cleared the gate. I flipped the lights and sirens on. I hung a right and took the alley expressway to 25th street. I took a left on 25th on two wheels. At J Street, I hit the cruiser's whoop, whoop to get the pedestrians moving in the crosswalk. The emergency sensors on J Street for first responder vehicles turned the traffic lights green all the way to Mercy Hospital. It took less than three minutes to get to the hospital, but it felt like an eternity. I kept glancing in the rear-view mirror at Connolly holding Sam, wrapped in his arms like a small child. Connolly was talking to Sam in a calm, warm voice, repeatedly saying, "Hold on, Sam, Roxxy is getting you help. Hold on, Sir." Siren's blaring, I turned left into the emergency lane, coming to a screeching halt under the portico behind an ambulance where a paramedic was loading a gurney. All in one motion, I threw the car in park, stomped on the e-brake, hit the siren switch, jumped out of the cruiser, and yelled, "Man down, bring that thing over here." Running around the back of the car, yanking the door open, and helping Connolly out with Sam in his arms. Connolly gently laid Sam on the gurney. I was running alongside the gurney barking out vitals and wounds. As the door that read "Hospital Personnel Only Beyond This Point" was closing, the paramedic said, "We'll take care of him, ma'am." His kind eyes gave me a glimmer of hope.

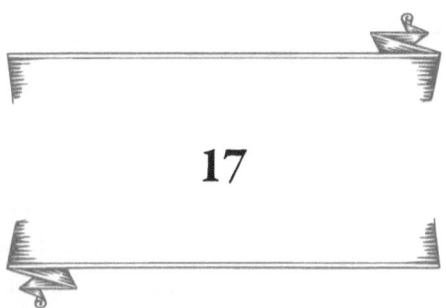

17

I STOOD IN THE BLEAK hospital hallway with the scent of heavy-duty cleansers, staring at the door that read "Hospital Personnel Only Beyond This Point." I was seething, replaying everything in my mind from when I parked the van in the garage to when the kind paramedic said, "We will take care of him, ma'am." Quietly talking to myself, "What am I missing? Think! Roxxanne" Starting at the beginning again as if I hit the rewind on an old VCR. As my pager buzzed on my hip, I heard Poppy's voice, "Go back farther, Red Roxx Foxx." I whispered, "Go back farther?" My pager buzzed again. I looked at the number. Two 911 pages from Mrs. Whack-a-Noodle Dentist. I exclaimed with a growl and hucked my pager at the fucking door that read "Hospital Personnel Only Beyond This Point." As the battery cover flew off the back of the pager, I heard Poppy again, "Go back farther." I realized the meaning of what Poppy said. The surveillance! I replayed the four days of the surveillance, and there it was, in plain sight.

On the fourth and final day of the surveillance, The snoozeville Dentist pulled out of the parking lot next to the office. He drove his usual route onto Broadway and made an immediate right on Land Park Dr. I waited for a beat, then pulled off the curb of Broadway and made the right on Land Park Dr. As I passed the parking lot where the nearly comatose Dentist exit, I caught a glimpse of a black SUV. I kept replaying it. I follow at a comfortable distance, expecting the boring-ass dentist to go straight home to the crazy-ass wife. As expected, as I drive by, I see the garage door open as he pulls into the driveway. I check my rear-view mirror to confirm he completes the action, and I see the black SUV two blocks back. I continue the replay, winding through the neighborhood of the Pocket Area. I make my way to I-5 north to go downtown. I look over my shoulder to merge onto the interstate from Florin Road. I see a white big-rig with the name TAG on the upper cab with black, red, and blue decals. I stomped on the accelerator to get out of her way. I put my blinker on to move over a lane before my lane turned into an exit-only ramp for Highway 50 East. I look over my shoulder and change lanes. I check my rearview mirror. "There! The black SUV is three cars back."

I loudly said, "Fuck!" I picked up the pieces of my pagers and looked at the number again. I felt someone watching me. I turned around to find Connolly watching me with an oddly quizzical expression. I asked, "How long have you been standing there?" "About the time you asked yourself what you're missing." He said in a sweet, understanding tone. I put a hand on my hip, with a bit of tude. Said, "So pretty much all of it, well ok then! I guess it's been nice knowing you." Connolly said in the same sweet, understanding tone, "I'm sorry, I just didn't want to interrupt. It seemed like you were working something out." I said, "Oh! With tear-filled eyes. Usually, this is where most guys bail." He cupped my face in his giant hands, using his thumbs to wipe away my tears, gently kissing me, "I'm hurt you didn't notice I'm not like most guys." I wrapped my arms around his waist, buried my face in his chest, and begged forgiveness for not noticing he was a glutton for punishment.

We walked back to the ER waiting area. Connolly badged the nurse and said, "We just brought in Samuel Washington. Roxxanne Foxx is his sister. Are there any updates on his condition?" I stood beside Connolly with my mouth closed and let him do all the lying. I mean talking. My bloodshot eyes and red face must have convinced the admittance nurse because she gave us an update. She said he was stable and the doctor would be out to talk to us. I thanked the nurse and told her we would be waiting in the hallway. Once, we found a couple of seats with a bit of privacy. Connolly said, "Ok! After you told me you had an eidetic memory during that first interview, I looked it up. I know what it is, but I don't know how it works. What did you remember?" I said, "It's like anyone's memory. The difference is I can recall in vivid detail. The best way I can explain it, my memory is like a video. I can replay it like a movie, watch it, and see vivid details I didn't originally pay attention to." He asked, "That is what you did today? You replayed the events of the shooting?" "Yes," I said. "I replayed from the shooting to the time those doors over there shut in my face. I wasn't getting anywhere. Then I heard my Poppy's voice say, "Go back farther" then I got a 911 page from that crazy Dentist's wife I worked for on the surveillance. I was trying to figure this out, and I got a second page and lost my temper. Poppy said, "Go back farther" I realized he meant to replay the surveillance. When I did, I saw when and where the black SUV started tailing me. They were in the Dentist's parking lot, and I got a glimpse of them there after I completed the surveillance at the Dentist's house in the Pocket Area. Then again, when I was on I-5 heading downtown to park my van. I don't know if the surveillance is connected or if that's where they surveilled me?"

Connolly asked, "What can you tell me about your client and the surveillance?" "You mean other than the fact she is bat shit crazy? She hired me for four-day surveillance to see if her husband was cheating on her. Loony Toons believed he was unfaithful. My standard line is if you think your spouse is cheating, they probably are. They usually hire me, spending a couple of grand to confirm what they already know. Not this time; you could set your watch to his routine. He leaves the house at exactly seven in the morning, drives straight to the dentist's office, where he remains until five o'clock sharp, then drives the same route at exactly the speed limit, straight home. All four days were the same." Connolly said, "Who does that? No variation in the route, no stopping, and no speeding. It's as if he is trying not to catch anyone's attention."

The doctor walked out of the no-admittance doors to look for us. He looked at Connolly and said, "Detective, are you injured?" Both Connolly and I looked at Connolly. Connolly said, "Oh!" Looking down at his shirt. "It isn't my blood. It's Sam's blood. How is he?" The doctor said, "You should get cleaned up." And walked back behind the doors and reappeared with scrubs and a plastic bag. He said, "Sam is doing well. Thanks to you for getting him here so quickly. He was bleeding internally just above his kidney on his left side. He had three exceedingly small bruises on his abdomen, indicating the injury was from something that hit him with great force that didn't puncture the skin. We made a small incision and repaired it microscopically." I asked, "Can we see him?" The doctor said, "He is still sedated but should be coming around soon. I'll have the nurse come get you when he is awake." He smiled a tired smile. Without another word disappeared behind the doors. I looked at my watch and said, "Damn! We have been here for three hours."

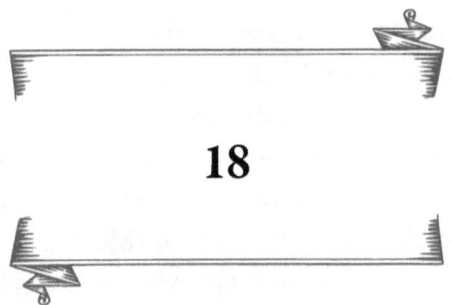

18

"HAVE YOU HEARD HOW the search for Maggie is going?" "No, it would help to talk to Sam to get more details. I'll check in with dispatch as soon as I get cleaned up. Maybe Sam will be awake by then, so we can talk to him." Connolly stood and kissed me on the cheek. "I'm going to find the men's room. I'll be right back."

I was lost in deep thought when I heard a southern drawl. "Well, ain't you a sight for sore eyes, my sister from another mister. I just knew it was you when I got instructed to let Miss Foxx know when her brother Samuel Washington was awake." Using her two fingers to make air quotes when she said, Brother. Like a schoolgirl, I squealed, "Jack, What the hell are you doing here?" Jackie is like a sister, but other than both of our hair is a shade of red, hers flaming red, mine dark red, we look nothing like blood sisters. She's five foot, nothing on a good day, and ninety-eight pounds soaking wet. Her skin is flawless and creamy, with snow-white perfection.

On the other hand, I tan to a dark brown and someday will remind myself of it when I'm old and wrinkled. We hugged, and I repeated, "What the hell are you doing here? And why didn't you tell me you were here?" She put her hand up as a stop sign and said, "Girl! I have been in this town for three weeks, and I have been trying to find a way to locate you, but you don't have a phone listing, you don't have Facebook, Instagram, or Tweet." I laughed and hugged her again and said, "You mean Twitter, right?" We were giggling. I said, "Old habits die hard." when Connolly walked up and cleared his throat, "Ladies! Keep it down. This is a hospital, after all." Then smiled a heart-melting smile and winked at me. Jack said, "Damn sugar are you with this luscious man?" I said, "Jack, this is Connolly, and don't even think about it." "Not to worry, honey. I can tell he has his sights set on you. Besides, I've always had a crush on that hunky Mulatto lying in that bed in there. You call brother." She used her fingers again for air quotes and laughed. Jack said, "Come on now, let's go see brother Sam."

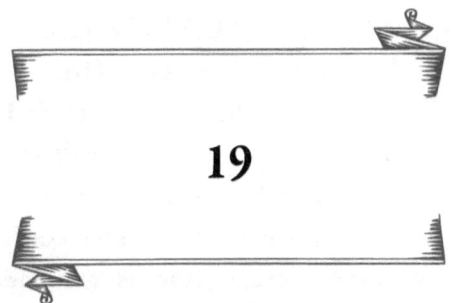

19

CONNOLLY AND I FOLLOWED Jack through the doors that read "Hospital Personnel Only Beyond This Point." Jack's flaming red hair pulled back into a long ponytail, swinging side to side as she strolled through the halls of her ward. She was the best nurse I have ever watched stitch up wounded warriors. She exudes confidence, and that's how it comes across, not as arrogance, simply confidence. Her patients felt it. They knew they were going to be okay if Jack were their nurse. She opened the door to a private room. I glanced at her and quietly asked, "Is this your doing? putting Sam in a private room." She was batting her eyes, fanning herself, saying in the syrupiest southern voice she could muster up, "Why I forever have no idea what you are talking about." I kissed her on the cheek and said, "I love you, Jack." She said, "Honey, I love you too. Let me know if you need anything. I need to go make my rounds." I sat down on the edge of the bed and quietly said Sam's name. He opened one eye, then the other. He was blinking his eyes, trying to blink the fog away. He said in a low, hoarse voice, "I've been waiting for you. I need to tell you what happened. Three men took Maggie. One was short and skinny, he looked like a bird face, with a hooked nose, but I broke his beak. The other one was big, and he had a silver hand with three hooks for fingers. They had matching tattoos of a human heart. It had an arrow through it with a snake wrapped around it. But I bit the head of the snake off the big one. He hit me with his hooked fingers. Roxxy, you have to find Maggie. She's my little girl. Please find her." "Sam, Sam?" I looked at Connolly and said, "He's out."

I looked Sam over, his body battered. I picked his hands up and inspected his knuckles. His knuckles busted open and swollen. "Looks like Sam got his fair share of licks in," Connolly said. I looked up at Connolly. "Sam's a scrapper," I said with a smile. Connolly and I walked out of Sam's room; Jack was leaning against the nurse's station, writing in a patient's chart. "He's asleep!" Jack said, "I'm surprised he stayed awake as long as he did. They cranked a lot of drugs into his system." I asked, "You still carry the little notebooks in your bra?" "Honey, just like you, old habits die hard." She said. I put my hand out, palm up, and she reached into her bra and pulled out a notebook. I used to tease her. Most of her weight was in her boobs. I wrote my pager number in her notebook and handed it to her. "Put the little symbol you used to use, so I know it's you."

I kissed her cheek. She hugged me with a big squeeze and said, "I love you, don't worry about Sam. I'll take good care of him. You go put those sumbitches in the ground." She looked at Connolly putting one hand on her hip and the other pointing a finger in his face. "I like you, Connolly, but you better have my girl six. If anything happens to her, your gonna have to answer to me." Connolly said, "Yes, ma'am, and if you need to get ahold of Roxxy faster than the pager method, here's my card. I'm not leaving her side." I said, "Oh, brother! Bye, Jack."

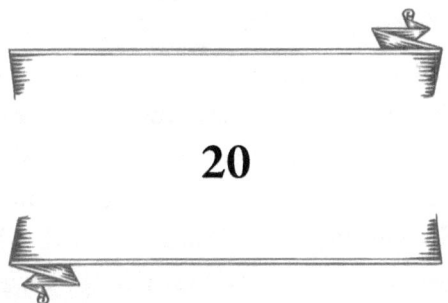

20

WE WALKED OUT OF THE Emergency Doors. Connolly had moved his cruiser off to the side, parking where the patrol officers park when they bring a suspect to get patched up before they book them into jail. Before we reached the car, all hell broke loose with Connolly's phone. He received a half dozen text messages with a little bling, bling. He got voice messages with a ding, ding, ding, and his phone was ringing. He looked at the caller's I.D. "It's Juanita! Hello?" I only understood "Si Chica" as Connolly was talking a mile a minute in a beautiful Spanish dialect.

The conversation went on for a good five minutes. Connolly raised his voice as the conversation got heated. Then I heard a couple more words I recognized "Mi Familia, adios" He hung up the phone. His eyes were dark coffee brown. "Hot Tamale, that was sexy as hell, an Irish boy speaking the beautiful Spanish language. Where did you learn to speak like that?" His eyes lightened as he smiled and said, "My last two years of higher education were in Spain. Get in. We need to go to the county morgue. Patrol found two bodies, a young female on the riverbank and a male body behind The Tower." My heart dropped, "Maggie?" He shook his head.

"I don't know. Neither one had identification." I asked, "What makes them believe they are connected?" Connolly said, "The male victim has Russian Mafia prison tattoos from head to toe. The female had a note attached to her written to Sam, in Russian loosely translated, "You take one of mine, I take one of yours" When you worked at Folsom Prison, did they send you to training to interpret gang tattoos and the meaning of them?" "Yes, it was the one training I really enjoyed. It was fascinating and somewhat of a history lesson. The ritual of Russian tattooing began in Soviet Union prisons in the nineteenth century."

We piled into the car Connolly's phone started going off again. The sexy Spanish language was flying a hundred miles an hour. As he was talking, he threw the car in reverse and skidded back, then threw it in drive, ripping out of the hospital parking lot. He punched the end button and said, "We need to swing by your place so I can change. After we go to the morgue, I want to go to both crime scenes. I don't want to show up in scrubs." I said, "Ok, I have blood on my clothes, so I'll change too, and if you don't mind, I want to change cars too." Connolly nodded and shrugged his shoulder. He said, "I had Juanita check with the morgue. The Russian you shot is still there. The coroner said he is covered in prison ink as well. I was hoping you could look at both of their bodies. Maybe it will give us a better idea of who we are dealing with." "Ok, but I want to deal with the girl's body first. Doesn't the FBI or Sac PD have gang units with tattoo specialists?" I said. Connolly smiled his hunky smile and said, "Yes, but I want your take on them. You have a unique gift. I think your memory will serve us well."

Connolly turned left just before J Street turned from a two-way street to a one-way in the opposite direction. He continued down Alhambra through hooker row, passing the nasty Red Roof Inn, where they rent rooms by the hour. He hung a right onto Capital, then another right on 26th to make our way to the alleyway expressway. Three blocks from my gate Connolly stomped on the brakes. Veering to the right of the alley, behind a dumpster. I said, "Black SUV?"

He nodded, scrolling through the call history in his smartphone, clicked a number, and waited while it rang. It went to voicemail. He paused for a beat, then tapped the screen again. He said, "Agent Baxter, this is Detective Connolly with Sacramento PD. Yes, I'm fine. Yes, Miss Foxx is also well. The purpose of the call is to find out if you have a team sitting at Miss Foxx's house. Ok! Thank you, yes better safe than sorry."

Connolly pulled out from behind the dumpster, and another black SUV drove by on 25th street, heading south. My spider sense went off like a five-alarm bell, and I hit the deck. I yelled, "That's not the FBI. That's him!" Connolly slowed to a crawl; he watched the SUV turn right two blocks down. As soon as he did, Connolly gunned it. He said, "Get the gate fob ready." I opened the gate a half block away, and Connolly skidded into the courtyard. I hit the button on the fob again. The gate closed before Connolly had his cruiser backed into the carport.

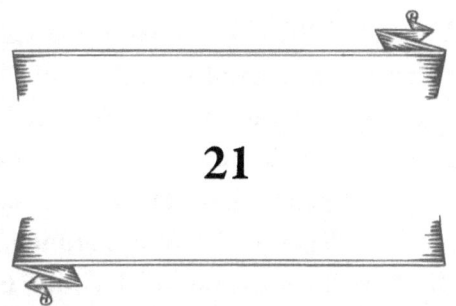

21

CONNOLLY CALLED IT in to dispatch. I asked, "Wouldn't it have been faster to use the radio?" "Yes, but he probably has a scanner, and I don't want the FBI team to leave their post. They might be as smart as a box of hair, but they serve a purpose watching your house," He said. "You're pretty smart for an Irish boy." "Wait a minute, aren't you an Irish girl?" "Precisely my point," I said. I blew a kiss, jumped out of the car, running up the stairs to the back door with him hot on my tail. He caught up to me at the alarm keypad inside the mud room. He pressed himself up against my ass, reaching around me while cupping my boobs. I hurriedly disarmed the alarm system. I broke out of his grasp, running for the stairs, taking them two at a time, tossing my t-shirt over my head, and hitting Connolly square in the face. When I hit the top of the stairs, I worked on the button and zipper of my jeans. Kicking my shoes off as I entered my bedroom and wiggling out of my jeans by the time I got to the shower. We each took a shower head at each end of the massive walk-in shower. Washing off the hospital and Sam's blood then met in the middle. He picked me up and pressed me against the marble wall. I wrapped my legs around him. On the opposite wall of the bathroom was a double sink vanity with a large mirror over it. As he moved rhythmically in and out, in and out. I watched his muscular back flexing and twitching with each thrust. With a raspy grown, he came following my lead. I unwrapped my legs from his waist and said, "That was the most intense quickie I have ever had." He smiled and said, "I wish we had more time, but I think I hear all hell breaking loose on the streets in your neighborhood." He stepped out of the shower and searched for his gym bag. I went to the dressing room to get dressed. I heard him say from the bedroom, "Roxx, where is my bag?" I yelled, "In here! I hope you don't mind. I unpacked your bag so your clothes wouldn't get jacked up with wrinkles." He kissed me on the forehead and said, "Not at all, thanks." We dressed. I grabbed my 45 cal from my jeans on the floor and tossed everything in a basket. Refreshed with a quickie and clean clothes, we headed to the garage.

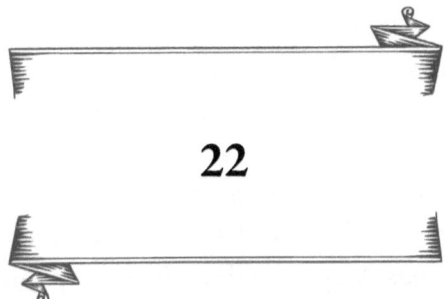

22

WE WENT DOWNSTAIRS. We heard sirens coming down the street in front of the house. We peeked outside just as a black SUV hauled by with four patrol cars in pursuit. I said, "Get Em, Get Em, Get Em!" Connolly followed me out to the garage, where I hit the remote, and the big heavy steel doors rolled up into a cylinder above the garage opening. Poppy installed the roll-up doors to allow for more headroom in the garage ceiling area for the big hydraulic car rack inside the garage. It's one of the many things Poppy and I had in common. We both love cool cars and hot bikes. Poppy was an avid rider who taught me to ride when I was nine. Each garage bay has two racks, one in front of the other, with two cars on each rack. Connolly entered the garage with his mouth open, staring at the rack and the cars. He said, "You have eight cars in here. I have never seen anything like this in person, I mean not in a private garage, only in museums or car shows. This is fucking badass!

I don't know what I like more. The car rack or the cars on the rack. Oh my god, is that a 1967 Cougar?" I said, "Yes, as a matter of fact, it is. I got it at a police-impound auction. The police seized it from a Mexican Cartel leader who was arrested and then killed by his people on his way to court. It has a 428 big block engine. With a four on the floor, manual transmission. And the suspension was replaced with the Cadillac SRT racing suspension. The front end was lowered just a little. And the glass, body, and tires are armored." Connolly was drooling. I said, "Get in. The only thing I added was tint to the windshield. Everything else was done." I pulled out from the bottom rack and out of the garage. I waited for the door to roll down and hit the remote to arm the alarm. Then I hit the button for the gate. I pulled out of the courtyard and waited for the gate. As I headed for 26th Street, the black SUV went racing by, but only two patrol cars were in pursuit. Just as I turned on 26th, we saw the two patrol cars come to a screeching halt to avoid running into the side of a garbage truck. The black SUV kept hauling ass down 26th. I told Connolly, "Hold on, baby" I dropped to second gear, and we slid around the tail end of the garbage truck like "Smokey and the Bandits," missing the garbage truck by a

hair. We caught up to the SUV on 26th street, under the elevated part of Highway 50, with its front doors wide open. I stopped in the middle of the road. In a split second, the SUV, Connolly, and I were surrounded by a dozen patrol cars.

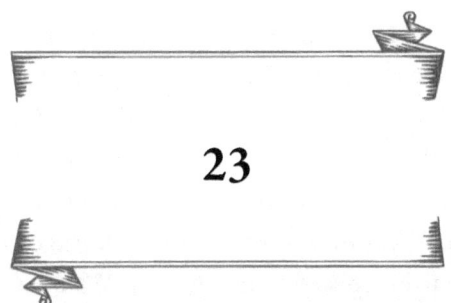

23

I TURNED OFF THE COUGAR, cranked the window down, and set my keys on the car's roof. I reached out the window and opened the door. Connolly was doing the same on his side. We exited the Cougar with our hands in the air and Connolly's badge in the palm of his hand, just to be on the safe side. We didn't want to be the victim of friendly fire by an adrenaline-spiked patrol jockey. We heard one of the officers say, "Holster your weapons, holster your weapons. They're one of us." Connolly looked toward where the voice was coming from with a big smile and said, "Hey, Brother!" Sergeant McNulty walked over to the Cougar and whistled a cat call to the car. And said, "Waz-up?" Connolly and McNulty shook hands and did a bro hug that turned into a full-body hug, patting each other on the back. McNulty grabbed Connolly by each side of his head and kissed him on the forehead. I was standing there with a big smile on my face, watching the exchange, when one of the patrol officers said, "Aw Geez Sarge, you two are carrying on like a couple of Nancy's, why don't ya get a room or something?" Laughter broke out. McNulty turned and said, "What's the matter, make ya uncomfortable seeing some man love? I'll cut you some slack cuz you don't know who this is. This here is a real hero."

One arm over Connolly's shoulder, patting his chest. He said, "If you're lucky, I'll buy you a pint one of these days and tell you the story. Now get back to work. Break up into three groups." He turned into Tommy Lee Jones from the movie "The Fugitive" barking out orders "Break into groups, knock on doors, Check every house, outhouse, doghouse, and hen house. Get CSI over here on this vehicle.

Check the business across the street for video. I want to know which direction they went and how they went there, by foot or car. Alright, move people."

Everyone went in different directions as if they had already worked out who would do what. Connolly introduced me to his Blue Brother, Tim McNulty. Connolly said, "Call me if you guys get anything. We are heading to the morgue." McNulty said, "Wow! You know how to treat a lady, taking her to the morgue. Alright, brother, take it easy. When you get a chance, let's meet up at Hooligans." "You bet, brother," Connolly said. We got in the car. I dropped it in first, ripped it down the street to Broadway, and hung a left towards Stockton Blvd.

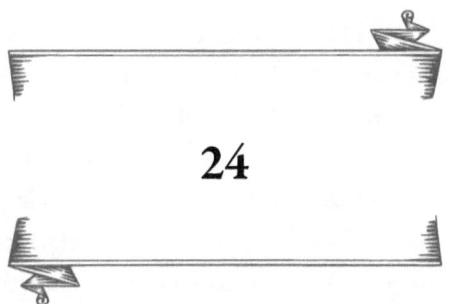

24

I PULLED UP TO THE gate of the county coroner's office, cranking the window down for Connolly to badge us in. The Deputy and Connolly briefly bantered about Connolly winning a bet and going to collect in the form of drinks at "Crawdads" on the water, a floating bar on the Sacramento River. Connolly pointed, "Park over there next to the meat wagon." We walked to the back entrance, where Connolly hit the intercom. A voice that sounded as if he gargled with ground-up asphalt for breakfast said, "Coroners" Connolly said, "Hey Doc, It's Connolly" "Hey Connolly, come on in." The door buzzed and, with a click, unlocked. "Awe, the smell of death and creepers," I said. Connolly threw an arm over my shoulder and tugged a little.

We went into an exam room. The stench hit me in the face like a sledgehammer. "Hey Doc! how's it hanging?" The coroner said, "A little to the left, how about you." As they bumped fists, Connolly introduced us, 'This is Roxx Foxx, Roxx, this is Doc." The Doc and I first shook hands, then hugged me and said, "Connolly is a good man, but if he ever steps out of line, let me know, and I'll take care of him." Connolly said, "Damn dude, two seconds, and you're already hitting on my girl."

Connolly looked at me and said, "Don't let this old fart fool you. He will try to sweep you off your feet if you aren't careful." I said, "I will keep it in mind, but you never know; I might want to be swept off my feet," and winked at Doc. "Doc, can we get to what we came here to do before you steal my girl? We need to make an identification on the white female they found by the river." He said, "She's over here. It always hurts when they are young." We walked over to a big metal table that looked like a shallow bathtub with drain holes at each end. Doc pulled the drape back, and we both said, "It's not Maggie." The young girl was about fifteen years old with shoulder-length dirty blond hair, ratted from not bathing for weeks. Doc said, "Damn! I was hoping we could put a name to this young girl." Connolly said, "We need to take a look at the two Skels with all the tattoos." "They are in the next exam room; I didn't want them here with this young lady." We walked next door to exam room four. There was one table in the middle of the room with a covered body. Doc uncovered him. I said, "Connolly, he does kind of look like a bird." I began examining the tattoos.

"See this one?" Pointing at the tattoo of a human heart. With an arrow through it and a snake wrapped around the arrow. On the head of the snake was a dunce hat and a small number five over the hat. I asked Doc, "Can I see the other male decedent with the tattoo like this one?" Doc walked over to a bank of drawers and pulled one of the drawers open. I looked at the man lying in the drawer. He had the human heart with an arrow through it, and wrapped around it was a snake. There was a crown on the head. The crown had five points. Over the third point of the crown was the number three. I went back to the table to compare the tattoos. Connolly and Doc watched my process without saying a word to me or to each other. Walking back and forth, I concentrated on one tattoo at a time and compared them on each man. When I completed the examination of each of the men's tattoos, I said. "The two men are related.

See the human heart tattoo? This tattoo here is their "Suit," which indicates their status. Each man has one, but the one with the Bird Face is a lower family member, maybe an idiot brother. The dunce hat is his service record. Most likely, he screws up jobs. The Bird Face also has a "Cat," which often means he is a thief, as in a cat burglar. And this one, pointing to "KOT," means he has been in prison several times. The eye on his stomach means he is gay, which can also explain the dunce hat. In this case, I think the human heart indicates they are blood-related, not just "thief in law," possibly because of being gay. His rank within the family is lower, not just in age. *Thanks to yours truly*, the one without a face has a "star" on his knees, which means he will kneel to no one. He also has a set of eyes on his chest, which usually means "watching over you." I think he watches over Bird Face, the family screw-up. I didn't get a look at his face when they were shooting at me. Based on his stature, I'm almost a hundred percent certain Bird Face is the man in the back seat of the SUV that was shooting at me.

Connolly asked Doc, "What was the cause of the death of Bird Face?" Doc said, "Somebody shoved his nose into his brain." I said, "Sam said he broke his beak." Connolly asked, "Roxx, you know either one of them?" I said, "I know the tattoo, but neither of these two men. Their body types don't match the man I knew with this tattoo. He is about six or seven inches taller than either of these men. I think he is the other guy who attacked Sam. I'd bet the Cougar on it." Connolly asked, "How do you know?" I said, "An educated guess at this point, but Sam described the other as big, and he had a silver hand with three hooks.

When I worked at Folsom State, a gang fight broke out. The COs were trying to break it up, and the big one Sam described was about to shiv one of the COs. I winged him from the tower. Took his hand off between the wrist and elbow." Doc said, "We got some evidence from the scene when this one came in. It's a chunk of flesh." I asked, "Can I see it?" Doc took a small tray out of a fridge and set it on the table. The piece of flesh was facing up. On it was a Snakehead wearing a crown with a small number four over the fourth crown point. I asked, "Doc did you have a chance to run the DNA on this and the two others?" Doc said, "Yes, but the results won't be in for a while. The two men's blood type and the piece of the flesh are all the same." "Okay, we have a good lead on some of the players, but it still doesn't add up. Why now? Why put a hit on you now? Bird Face is a screw-up; he didn't order the hit," Connolly said.

I said, "Who is the number one and number two on the crown? We know number three is no face. Number four Is the enforcer. Number five is the screw-up," Connolly said, "Excellent questions. Maybe the crime scene will tell us something. Thanks, Doc. We need to hit the river" when we get this wrapped up." Doc said, "Anytime, Son! I love you, keep your head down and call your mother. She worries to death over you." I said, "It was a pleasure meeting you. I wished it was under better circumstances."

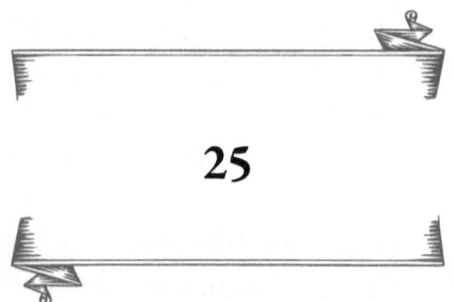

25

WE GOT IN THE COUGAR, and I smacked Connolly on the arm. "Why didn't you tell me we were going to see your dad?" Connolly tried to duck and chuckled. "I didn't want it to get weird. Not everyone can handle my dad being the "Coroner." You know, the guy who works on dead people? I don't see him as the guy who works on dead people. I look at him as the best investigator, I know, but civilians get creeped out." "I'm not the typical civilian." He said, "Clearly, you aren't typical in anything." "Flattery will not get you out of the doghouse." He smiled his big, gorgeous smile, filling the passenger seat with his 6'5" stature. He turned in the seat the best he could, wrapping his fingers at the nape of my neck. He leaned over and sweetly said, "I'm sorry," and kissed me on the cheek. I said, "Okay, that did it. You are officially out of the doghouse." He said, "Let's go to The Tower first."

We backtracked to Broadway. The Tower sits on a pie-shaped lot on Broadway and Land Park Drive. As we were waiting for the light to change to turn onto Land Park Dr, I glanced over at it the Dentist's Office. I nodded in the direction of the dentist's office and said, "That's the dentist's office I was sitting on when "No Face" and "Bird Face" started tailing me. They were in that parking lot the first time I saw them." The light turned green. I made the left turn onto Land Park, then an immediate right into the back parking lot of the beautiful ornate building of The Tower. Tower Records used to be in a small pharmacy next to The Tower Theater, where it got its name.

We parked outside of the yellow crime scene tape. When we got out of the car, I said, "Growing up, I would ride my bicycle to this place to catch an old movie for a quarter. Then next door to Tower Records to buy a record or two. I could get lost in there for hours." Connolly said, "We have so much in common. I'm surprised we didn't know each other." I said, "Well, I went to an all-girls catholic school." He laughed and said, "l went to Jesuit Catholic School. Doc and Mom still live near there, in the house I grew up in." I said, "The only reason I come here now is the Tower Cafe. It's amazing. They are famous for their French Toast. We have to go there one of these days. Maybe catch an old flick. Did you know Tower Theater is the oldest continuously running picture place?"

I stood at the tape, taking in the entire crime scene. I saw something on the ground under a dumpster. It didn't have an evidence marker next to it. I asked Connolly, "What is that?" Pointing to the dumpster, "It's under the right side." Connolly said, "Officer did you get this?" He squatted down, pointing to it with his pen. The officer did the same, looking closely at it. The officer put an evidence marker next to it, then a ruler, taking several pictures from different angles. Then rolled the dumpster out of the way and took several more photos. I asked Connolly, "What is it?" He said, "Looks like part of a human ear." I cuffed my ear and said, "What!" He said, "Haha, very funny."

I was standing outside the tape. I moved to the right of the scene, to the sidewalk along Land Park. Looking at the scene from a different perspective, I visualized the attack on Sam. I was picturing how he fought ferociously to protect Maggie. Quietly talking to myself, "Maggie, where are you? Hang on, girl, we're going to find you, and I'll put the son of a bitch in the ground." Standing on the sidewalk along Land Park, I felt eyes on me. I paid more attention to the faces of the crowd of onlookers that formed near the scene. I looked at each face individually, concentrating on their body language. No one stood out to me, and no one paid attention to me either. They were too enthralled by the police activity behind the famous Tower Records building. The eyes I felt on me wasn't coming from the crowd. I looked down the street to my left towards William Land Park. Nothing but the affluent homes along the tree-lined street. I turned to my right, slowly walking towards the corner of Broadway and Land Park. Across Broadway was the parking lot of the dentist's office. The lot was utterly deserted. No getaway cars, no black SUVs, and no one in sight but the closer I got to the corner of the intersection, the more intense the feeling of someone watching me. I stood there looking at the empty dentist parking lot and the dark office windows when I heard someone calling my name coming from a familiar voice.

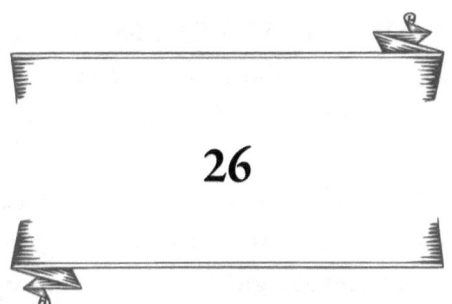

26

I LOOKED TOWARD WHERE I had parked the spy rig just a few days earlier. Walking towards me was my favorite hooker, Shelby. Shelby is a fifty-one-year-old hooker with a serious meth habit. She's thin with shoulder-length curly blond hair. I met Shelby while working on a missing person case a few months ago. Almost everyone gave up on the missing troubled teenage girl I was looking for except her only living relative, her older sister. Her sister was desperate to find her but was broke as hell. To make it official, I charged her a dollar for my retainer. It's not like I need the money. I pretty much work to keep myself busy and out of trouble. A fat lot of good it's done for me lately. At least on staying out of trouble. I know this area like the back of my hand. I know most of the flop houses where the prostitutes crash or get high when they aren't on a corner. Shelby was reluctant to help me to find Susie. She said the people who have her aren't like regular pimps. They are vicious and use young girls, sometimes little girls. She told me they don't use the corners because the girls are so young. They use websites like Red Door. When I showed Shelby a picture of Susie with her sister, Shelby started crying. She asked, "Who is the other girl in the picture?" I told her, "It was her sister. She hired me to find Susie." She said, "So, someone loves her enough to look for her?" I said, "Yes, and to pay me to help." With tears running down her hardened face, Shelby said, "I wish I had that when I was her age. Maybe things would've been different."

Although she was consumed with fear of the men behind the Red Door, she agreed to help me. With Shelby's help, I had Susie home with her sister within a couple of hours. "I hardly recognize you, Shelby. You look amazing. How are you doing?" Shelby said, "I'm doing great. Ever since the thing with Susie, I've been clean. I have a job here at Tower Café." Hooking a thumb over her shoulder. I asked her, "Is that the backpack I gave you?" Astonished, she was still carrying it. She said, "Yeah!" with a big smile that showed she was missing a few teeth from her hard life on the streets, living a lifetime on meth. She lifted her sleeve to expose her shoulder, showing me a scar the size of a tennis ball.

I said, "Wow! that really healed nicely." She said, "Thanks for the medicine you put in this backpack." With a happy little giggle, she proudly opened the backpack. She said, "I don't go anywhere without it. I keep it stocked with the ointment you gave me, wipes, hand sanitizers, aspirin, rubbers, and bottled water. The only thing I added to the supplies is tampons. As you did for me, I pay it forward to the girls out here." At that very moment, I thanked God I was wearing dark sunglasses to hide the tears welling up in my eyes. Shelby looked at her watch and said, "Shoot, I'm going to be late for my shift." Before I knew it, she wrapped her arms around me and said, "Thank you for saving Susie and me." Then she was off in a flash inside the cafe.

Walking back to the crime scene, I paused momentarily, looking at the empty dentist parking lot. The feeling of someone watching me has stopped. I had a wide range of emotions going on inside me, from the eerie feeling of the eyes on me and the complete sense of fulfillment with Shelby. Connolly met me halfway to the scene. He hugged me and said, "I don't know how to say this. I'm sure I'm going to mess it up, I know you can take care of yourself, but you scared the hell out of me. One minute you're standing there doing your thing, and the next, your gone. Can you please let me know before wandering off for a half hour when crazy Russians are trying to kill you?" I started to pull away with defensive thoughts of how dare you. Then Connolly took my face in his freakishly large hands, looking me in the eyes, and said, "I just found you!" How could I possibly get defensive? Instead, I wrapped my arms around his waist, buried my face in his chest, and said, "I'm sorry." He smiled, saying, "I'm done here for now. How about you? Are you ready to go to the other scene?" I nodded without saying anything and started to walk to the car. Connolly draped an arm over my shoulder and asked if I was okay. I nodded again and said, "I'll tell you in the car. Would you mind driving?" tossing the keys to him. He was like a giddy teenage boy getting a new hot rod. We got in the car, and before turning over the big v8, he got profoundly serious. In his severe low cop voice, he said, "Ok, tell me what you learned."

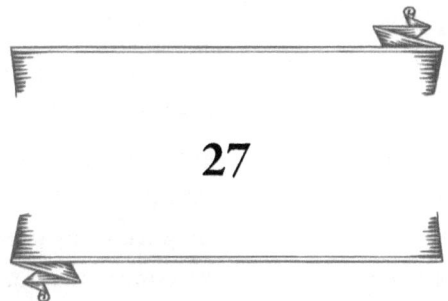

27

I TURNED SIDEWAYS IN my seat; I started rattling off everything. I explained how in the early years of my career in the USAF, the Security Forces were the Military Police. Both on and off the air bases. As part of my early assignments, I trained in the traditional law enforcement unit. Crime scene investigations weren't as prevalent as in a city like Sacramento but more common than one would like to think. One of the things I did was make a memory stamp. Connolly glanced at me and said, "I read about that when I researched eidetic memory. Is that what you were doing today?" "Yes, my method is to take a memory stamp from multiple perspectives. After finding the piece of an ear, I moved to the sidewalk on Land Park. I took in the entire scene. Then, as I was standing there, I felt someone watching me. I studied each face at the scene. I watched their body language. Whoever it was, it wasn't anyone at the scene. From that vantage point, I can see the dentist's office. I walked to the corner, and I swear the feeling got stronger, but the office was completely dark with no signs of life, and the parking lot was completely empty. Then I ran into Shelby outside of Tower Cafe." Connolly asked, "Who is Shelby?" I told him about Shelby and Susie, how Shelby now has a job, still has the backpack I gave her, and how she pays it forward. I told him how young Susie was, and they sold her on the Red Door website. "Did you know Sacramento was one of the largest human trafficking hubs in the nation? Doc said the dead girl had severe vaginal tearing and ligature marks on her wrist. I think this is somehow related to Susie's case. Maybe the men behind the Red Door are finally getting back at me for taking away one of their money makers." Both Connolly and I said, "It doesn't make sense!" I pinched him on the arm and said, "Pinch poke, you owe me a coke." Connolly laughed and said, "What are you twelve? "I said, "Thank you," he said, "For what?" "I have never been able to talk about how this crazy head of mine works before. I mean, no one I like the way I like you. Jack and Sam get me, but I like you differently." Connolly's cheeks blushed a little as he spoke. He stammered his words, saying, "I, I really like you too." and took my hand in his. His touch was warm and comforting. We finished the trip across town in silence, holding hands.

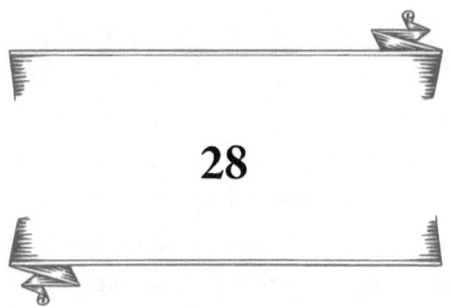

28

WE PULLED INTO ST FRANCIS High school; we parked in the same spot as we did just the day before. The Hornets Stadium parking lot was packed with police cars and various news channels this time. The skinny little runner chick from channel 3 KQRA knew Connolly's name on sight. The illogical green-eyed devil reared its ugly head. I'm not usually the jealous type, but then again, I've never felt this way about anyone before. She ran over, talking over the crowd, sticking a microphone in his face, "Detective Connolly, what can you tell us about the body found early this morning on the bank of the American River?" Connolly turned on his professional cop voice he said, "This is an ongoing investigation, no comment at this time."

She turned her attention towards me with microphones and cameras in my face. She said, "Ma'am do you work for the police department? Do you have a comment?" I looked straight into the camera as if I were looking at the killer and said, "No, I don't work for the police department. I want the person or persons responsible for this to know we will catch you." Connolly put his hand on the small of my back. He guided me through the reporters' gauntlet with their barrage of questions.

We made our way to the crime scene tape at the trail's edge. I asked, "How in the hell did they find out about this?" Connolly said, "They have their network of confidential informants within the department. They also listen to police scanners. My biggest problem with it is your face being on camera." I said, "Why? Do I have something stuck in my teeth? Or is it because of my crossed eyes?" I scrunched up my face crossing my eyes. He stifled a laugh, then said, "Stop. It's inappropriate to laugh at a crime scene. And you have a target on your back." "I know, but I'll be damned if they are going to scare me into hiding." We walked into a clearing.

There were a dozen or so CSI technicians collecting evidence. A couple of CSIs measured the surrounding area where the young girl's body was found. I asked, "Have they identified the girl?" "Yeah, while we were at The Tower, Doc sent me a text saying she was in the missing child databank. She's from Modesto." "I remember hearing about her. She was a great student, on track to go to Stanford." Connolly continued, "She disappeared on her way home from the park about seven months ago." "I don't get the note. Didn't it say you take one of mine, I take one of yours?" Connolly said, "It was in Russian. Maybe the translation is off a little." "I guess, but it's weird." I stood on the river levy at the edge of the scene, looking at the area. I moved downriver a little to take in the scene from another advantage point.

Walking closer to the river, I heard some rustling in the bushes, then two filthy men jumped out and grabbed me. I kicked one in the nuts and throat and punched the other one. I yelled for Connolly, "Help! I need some cuffs." The guy I kicked in the nuts wasn't going anywhere anytime soon. My big steel-toed Harley boots connected so hard he may need to have his nuts surgically removed from his throat. He was rolling around on the ground, moaning and groaning. I had the other one on his stomach with his arms behind his back shoved up between his shoulders. Connolly came running over, "What the hell happened over here?" I said, "These two assholes tried to grab me." Every time the guy I was holding squirmed, I dug my knee into his kidney. Connolly yelled at a couple of patrol officers, "Hey, come over, take these two idiots down to the station for attempted kidnapping, and assault with the intent of grave bodily harm."

One of the officers said while laughing, "Ok, Detective, but it looks like she did grave bodily harm to these two clowns. That dumbass may never see his nuts again." Connolly gave me a hand and said, "Look at you. I can't take you anywhere without you rolling around and getting all dirty." Brushing off the dirt and foxtails. I smiled, "I'll do just about anything to get you to brush the dirt off my ass." Connolly snuck a quick kiss. "They tried to grab you with about fifty cops around." I said, "Just goes to show how dumb they are." Connolly said, "Dumb and desperate. Desperation can be deadly." I said, "So can stupidity."

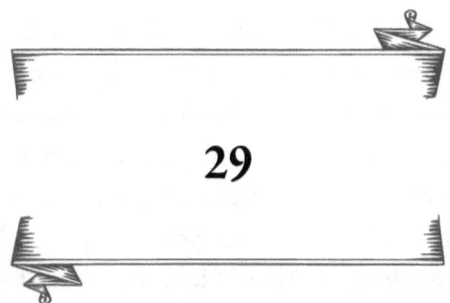

29

CONNOLLY'S PHONE DINGED with a text. He read the text looking up at me. "It's Jack. She even texts with a southern drawl. She said she saw your face plastered all over tv, she's fixin to kick my ass, and if anything happens to you, I was up shit creek without a paddle. Also, Sam is awake and is asking for you." I said, "So, you ready to roll? I have a couple of questions for Sam." He said, "Yeah, I just need to talk to CSI Geek.' I raised my eyebrow. Connolly laughed and said, "Sorry, He's a buddy, I call him "CSI Geek" to his face, and he calls me an "Armed Dick," sometimes "AD" for short." I said, "Okay, as long as I don't get a nickname." "Too late! It's 'Mizz Hot Foxx' Putting up his hands in defense, "It wasn't me; it was Juanita."

I said, "Well, if your gonna have a nickname, you might as well have a nice one. Poppy used to call me Red Roxx Foxx." Connolly stopped to talk to one of the CSIs, and they did some complicated handshake. On his way up to the top of the levy, Connolly yelled over his shoulder, "Hey Brother, don't forget you owe me a pint, Hooligans." CSI Geek said, "Yeah-Yeah, I'll see you there." We took a different trail to bypass the Hornets parking lot. Luckily, it seemed to have worked. As we crossed the street to St Francis, Connolly took my hand in his. He started handing me the keys, but I asked if he would drive. And on cue, there's the giddy teenager again. He plugged the key into the passenger door to unlock it, and the car alarm went off. I grabbed the hand he was using and dragged him away from the car. We ran as fast as we could, diving behind the CSI van as the car jumped about three feet in the air. Connolly said, "What the Hell?" Rolling over and sitting on his ass with his legs stretched out in front of him. I said, "I'm pretty sure the Cougar is gonna need a tow to the shop." As Connolly was sitting on the hot pavement, he put the palms of his hands to his head and cried out, "Not the Cougar!" I patted him on the back, reassuring "It'll be okay, she'll be okay, she's armored." He looked at me with disbelief. "She is? Wait, how did you know what was going to happen?" I took the key from his hand, holding it in front of his face. "This told me. This is a smart key. I told you about getting it from a police auction, and it used to be owned by a Mexican Cartel. He was extremely paranoid. There are sensors all over the car that talks to this key. See the chip right there? The sensors can detect the chemical makeup of C-4 or the frequency of a GPS tracking device and weight distribution. So, if someone tampers with the Cougar and the person doesn't have this key on their person. When the key is inserted into the door, it sounds a different alarm for what it has detected." Connolly said, "Holy Fuck!"

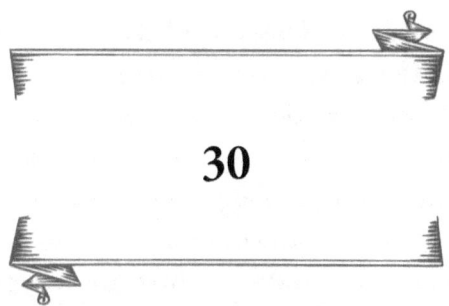

30

THE EXPLOSION WASN'T all that big, but it got the attention of the news channels across the street in the Hornets parking lot, along with the police working the perimeter of the crime scene. Someone called it in, and within minutes the hose draggers were there—any excuse to take their big shiny red trucks out.

We decided it would be best to use this to our advantage. We stayed out of the news media site. We released a bogus statement that read, "At this time, we are not releasing the identities of the victims involved in the explosion. Not until family members have been notified." It isn't a lie; they didn't say we perished. I was putting the pieces together in my head, watching the tow truck attempt to winch the car up on the flatbed from the back of the CSI van. The driver walked over to CSI Geek. He was handling the transport of the Cougar for Connolly in our absence. The driver told CSI Geek he had to call in for a more oversized flatbed. The Cougar was too heavy for his rig. A similar tow truck showed up, but this one was huge. Connolly was sitting across from me on a bench in the back of the van, talking to his lieutenant. He was giving him the rundown of the case and the plan moving forward. Hanging up with his lieutenant. He asked me, "So are you getting anywhere with this?" I smiled. "As a matter of fact, I think I am. It's been right there in front of my thick head from the beginning, but I need to talk to Sam first to be sure." He said, "Okay, tell me what you know so far." Just as I started to verbally vomit everything I knew, my pager quietly vibrated on my hip. Before I had a chance to reach for it, it vibrated again. The first page was Mrs. Looney Farm

Dentist, with a 911 page that sent chills up my spine. The second page was Pops, also a 911 page. "I need to get to the house. Pops paged. The other one is the dentist's wife." "I called Juanita. There's an unmarked unit on its way as we speak." Connolly sat on the bench next to me, draping his arm over my shoulder and kissing me on the head. "Holding up?" I said, "Yeah, but I'm just about fed up with this nonsense." CSI Geek popped his head in the door and said, "Your car is rolling to the lab; I'll take good care of it. Also, your ride is here." "Thank you, I appreciate it." Connolly asked, "Can you take us over to the Renegades parking lot and have a cruiser follow us there." "Sure, brother, hang tight. I need to let my crew know I'll meet them at the lab."

We pulled into the Renegades parking lot and did a quick Chinese fire drill. Connolly bumped fists with the officer from the unmarked cruiser as they passed each other. Then, in a flash, we were off.

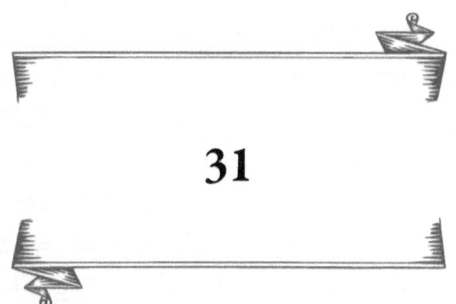

31

WE TOOK A COMPLETELY different route to the house than we had been. We went east on Folsom Blvd to Howe Ave, then passed Cal Expo to Highway 160. We entered downtown from the north, then hit the alley expressway. I hit the remote as Connolly hooked it into the courtyard. As Connolly was backing into the spot where the Cougar usually rested, I got another page from Pops. This one was two consecutive 911s. "Oh boy, I better get inside and call Pops. The page has two nine-elevens." We walked into the mud room, and it was all clear. No spooks had been in the house. We went to the vault to call Pops, "Hi Pops, no, I wasn't injured, but the Cougar will probably need to be shipped to Armormax to be re-wired, replace the sensors, and have the plates inspected, possibly replaced. We thought it might take the heat off if they believed I didn't survive. Uh-huh, no, what? Wait, Pops, I'm a civilian, recall? What the hell, Pops? I, I, Yes, Sir. Yes Sir, Thank you, Sir. Yes Sir," Connolly was listening to the one-sided conversation with eyes the size of silver dollars, "Yes, Sir, I would like to talk to him again. What the hell, pops a little notice would've been nice, Oh Ok!! I'll report to Beale at 0600. Does the team know I'm taking over? Ok, Thank you, Sir. I love you too," I sat the phone down and banged my head on the desk. Connolly's face was white as a sheep's. "Um! Was that the President of the United States you were just talking to?" With my forehead still stuck to the desk, I answered, "It was!" Connolly asked, "What was the recall thing about?" "I was called back to duty." I sat up. I used air quotes. "Temporarily" Oh, for fuck's sake, I don't want to do this." I took a long, deep-deep, cleansing breath and reached into the air. I did an imaginary scrotum pull. I shook it off and said, "It's time to pull up my big girl panties and quit whining." Connolly said with a shit-eating grin, "Um, I don't think you wear panties, just how I like it." He kissed the top of my head. Saying we need to roll over to the hospital before Jack kills me." I giggled, saying, "Look at you, a big ole boy like you scared of a little five-foot-nothing girl." He said, "Hell Yeah, I think she might be meaner than a junkyard dog. Besides, the first rule when a dude likes someone is to ensure you stay on the good side of their bestie." "Oh. Is that right? what about staying on my good side?" He stood me up, wrapping his arms around me and whispering in my ear, "Baby, all your sides are more than good." I buried my head in his chest, trying to get my stomach to stop doing flip-flops. I said, "Ok, enough of all this mushy stuff. We better get to the hospital before Jack kills us both. She'll make us wish we were in the car when it was a Mexican jumping bean."

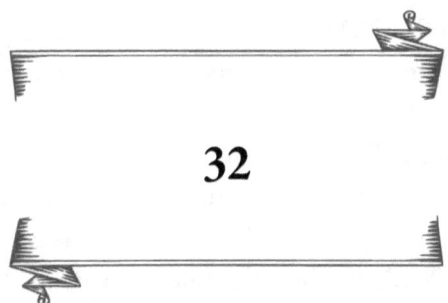

32

WE STARTED TO LEAVE the vault when I got another page from Mrs. Looney Tunes Dentist. I got an aching feeling when I looked at the page. Connolly asked, "Is it your Godfather?" "No, it's the Dentist's Wife. I don't have a good feeling about this. I need to call her." I called the number on the page, and the voice on the other end whispered, "hello?" Then the line went dead. I pulled the receiver back, looking at it. I hung up and dialed again. This time it was answered by a man with a strong Russian accent. I said, "Hello, I'm returning a call from this number." The Russian voice indignantly asked, "Is this Roxxy Foxx Private Investigator?" I said, "No, this is Homicide Detective Peterson, returning calls from Miss Foxx effects. To whom am I speaking?" Click!! I said, "Shit! He hung up." I called again, no answer, just a mechanical voice saying, "The number you dialed is not available and has not been set up for voicemail, goodbye." I said, "It's probably a burner phone, but can you run it?" Writing the number on a sticky note. "Whoever originally answered was whispering before getting disconnected." "Sure! I'll call Juanita on the way to the hospital. How did you know we have a homicide detective named Peterson?" I smiled, "I saw the nameplate on one of the cubicles at the department when I came to sign the statement after the shooting. I have no idea if the Detective is male or female. Hopefully, the Russian doesn't check it out any further." "You're in luck, Peterson is female, but she looks nothing like you. She's a curvy fireplug and would be as hot for you as I am. Well, maybe not as much as I am, plus Peterson is a player. She's a love and leavin' kind of girl." "Well, maybe this will lighten the heat from the Russians and give me time to get to Beale to assemble the team." He asked, "Can you tell me anything about the mission." I said, "Not really, but you already know what my standing orders were, but I have a feeling Ely Stanlogovich isn't the "Capture" kind of guy." "What's the connection with the Dentist's wife? How did Stanlogovich get her phone?" I said, "I think the Dentist and Stanlogovich are the same people. Craig said Stanlogovich went underground, probably by taking a new identity." Connolly said, "A Dentist, though? That requires school and license." I said, "Assuming the office is an actual Dentist's Office, when I called to get an appointment, the receptionist said they weren't taking on any new patients at this time. Thinking about it now, the receptionist didn't have an accent per se but spoke very deliberately and a little choppy."

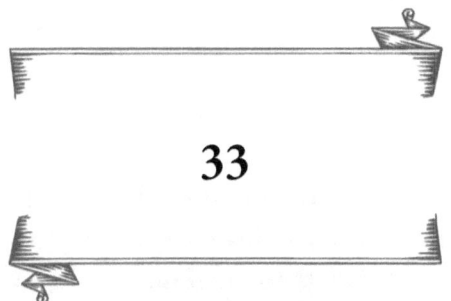

33

WE DROVE TO THE HOSPITAL in silence. Connolly seemed like he was lost in thought. I could almost hear the wheels turning in his head from the passenger seat of the unmarked cruiser. The silence was deafening. I finally found someone I could talk to, but now he seemed to be working things out in his head in his own way. Every investigator, worth anything, has their method. I talk to myself and replay the things I see. Some write notes. Some investigators bounce ideas off team members. Some sleep on them, and some internalize them. Connolly pulled the cruiser into a parking space at the hospital reserved for Law Enforcement.

I started to open the car door when he softly said, "Wait for a second, please. I need to say something to you." I said, "Uh oh! This doesn't sound good." His face was calm and sweet. His eyes darkened to dark chocolate. He smiled sweetly. "You are one of the most capable persons I know, but I'm worried." I said, "Oh! I thought this was going to be "this has been fun, but I'm out," talk." Turning in his seat as much as someone his size physically could. He cupped my chin, "I think I fell in love with you the moment I looked into your jade-green eyes."

I felt my stomach drop and my eyes tear up. "I'm a little scared." "I know it's moving fast, I get it, but I had to tell you how I felt before you left to go to Beale Airforce Base. Sometimes, you don't get a second chance to say how you feel. I don't know what to expect with you recalled to duty. I have never actually heard of such a thing. What you are about to do is dangerous at the bare minimum. I don't want to regret not telling you how I feel." I crawled over the console into his lap, kissing him. "I have never felt this way before, so I'm scared. I have never been in love with anyone until now. I promise I will come through on the other side of this." Kissing him and hugging him tighter than I have ever hugged anyone. "Thank you for being so supportive and open. Not only with your feelings but with how I am. I love you." He smiled and said, "We better get inside before Jack kills me."

Jack was at the nurse's station when we walked into the ward. She looked over her shoulder, spun on her heels, and put a hand on her sassy hip. "I told you if anything happened to her, you would have to answer to me. I thought for sure you two were goners. Until someone called to let me know you were okay." Connolly said, "Actually, Roxxy saved us both." Jack said, "No doubt! You wouldn't believe half the shit this Chic-a-dee has done. One time..." I interrupted, "Jack, we don't have time for war stories. I've been recalled for duty and have to report to Beale. How's Sam? Can we talk to him?" "Wait, you've been what? I've never heard of such a thing. You put your twenty in and retired." "I know it's a long story, but Pops called." "Oh, Darlin, you're screwed, blued, and tattooed. You ain't gonna say no to him. Well then, honey, come with me. Let's see Sam." We walked into Sam's room. His bed was empty, the IV stand was empty, and his hospital gown was lying on the floor.

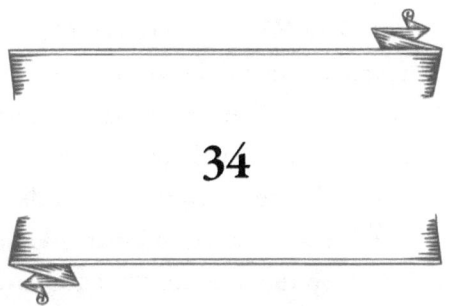

34

JACK CHECKED THE BATHROOM, checked his records, and stomped out of the room without a word. I could hear Jack say, "Y'all know where my patient from bed 138 is?" I couldn't hear their response, but I heard Jack say, "Lockdown Protocol, we have a code black." Jack entered the room like a red-headed Tasmania devil. "Sam's gone!" Then a voice on the intercom hanging around Jack's neck said, "Jack can you call security, please?" "For heaven's sake!" Jack walked to the phone hanging on the wall at the head of Sam's bed and dialed an extension. "This is Jack!" Jack was listening to the voice on the other end of the line, throwing a hand on her hip. "He did what? How do you know this? What exit was that? Ok, there are two detectives here. I'm sending them to see you. You show them that video, ya hear me?" Hanging up the phone with enough force to knock the base off the wall. "Sam's MIA. He made a call from this line to a 916 number, then strolled out of the east exit. Security has the number he dialed and the video waiting for you. Connolly, you find that boy and get him back here. He developed a low-grade fever, and the little turd snuck out when I went to get antibiotics ordered for him. That fever can be the beginning of an infection. You get him back here, ya hear?" Connolly simply said, "Yes, ma'am!" And he walked out of the room. I kissed Jack and started to follow Connolly. Jack spun me around, "Listen here, girl, you got your orders. You take those sumbitches out! And get back here safely." Hugging me tightly, "Alright now, go save the world." "Yes, ma'am!" Saluting a half-assed salute.

I caught up to Connolly as he came out of the security office. "The number Sam called was an Uber service." "Did they say where he went?" "No, we had the misfortune to get someone who is safety conscientious. She wouldn't give the information over the phone without proper identification." I looked at my watch and said, 'Where? I have time before I need to take off for Beale." He said, "The city marina at the end of Broadway."

We met the Uber driver in the parking lot of Sacramento City Marina. She was oddly pretty. A gothic girl of about twenty years old: her eyes were much older. This girl has seen some shit at her young age. She studied us as we walked over to her. She was leaning against her Prius. She said, nodding her chin in Connolly's direction and then towards me. "You're the cop? What are you?" I stepped into the girl's invisible bubble of personal space, looking into her eyes, "I can tell you've seen some shit in your life. You are smart enough to know when someone is bullshitting you. The man you dropped off is like a brother to me, I would die for him, and I don't have time for twenty questions. So where did you drop him?" The goth girl stared back at me for a moment, reading me, finally saying, "Here, I dropped him here. He went through that gate." Nodding towards a gate that led down to the moored boats in the City Marina. "Thank you! If you ever need anything, please page me, anything at all, anytime." Handing her my card with my name and pager number. She looked at the black card with bold red print and read, "Roxxy Foxx 916-956-8159, Thanks." Handing the card back to me, "I'll remember that and the number. Save the card for the next person and save a tree."

I said, "Repeat the number." She repeated, "916-956-8149, old school pager." I smiled and said, "Alright, Goth, Thanks!" Connolly fell into step with me to the gate Sam entered. Connolly was already digging in his pocket when I asked him, "Do you have a Knox key?" Looking over his shoulder as the Goth girl drove away in her white Prius with the Uber and Lyft stickers on the back of the hatchback. "What was up with that? You know her?" "No, but that girl has seen a lot of unpleasant things in her lifetime, and like me, she can remember it all in vivid detail." He nodded an understanding nod. When we got to the fuel dock, where the harbor master's office was located, we saw an older Sea Ray Sundancer with the name "Maggie" on its stern, getting up on plane as it was exiting Mariana's five-mile-an-hour zone.

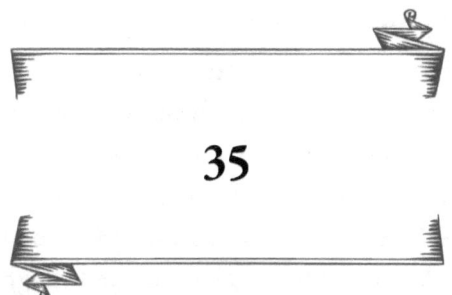

35

CONNOLLY POINTING, "There he is! he has a yacht?" "Damn! He talked about getting one, but I didn't realize he had." "The good news is I have some friends with the Sheriff's boat patrol unit" Connolly scrolled through his phone and clicked a number. "Hey Brother, you on a boat today? I need a favor. Can you stop and hold an older 410 Sundancer? Maybe 1995 to 1997, named Maggie, heading down river from the City Marina?" Connolly listened to the friend repeat the information, then said, "That's A-firm. Thanks, Brother, I owe you." We got back to the cruiser, and I received a page.

I read the phone number with a G9 code following the phone number. "It's Pops. Can I use your phone?" "Sure, but it's not a secure line." "I know it's ok. He gave me a code to contact immediately with whatever means I have available." I dialed the number "Sir, yes, Sir! It's Detective Connolly's phone. Yes, Sir, he has been instrumental in this situation. Yes, Sir, he has my six, Sir, Foxtrot Seven? Yes, Sir, I remember the location. Sir, that was twenty minutes ago. Yes, Sir, I'm two minutes out. Thank you, Sir. Okay, Pops, I love you too." Connolly was smiling and shaking his head, "Your conversations with him are the most bizarre one-sided conversation I have ever eavesdropped on; it's all business, then it's all family." I responded, "It's not unlike you and Doc. You two were like two old college buddies, then the whole dad and son interaction."

"Hmm, I guess you're right. Anyway, what's up?" "They got some intel about Ely Stanlogovich moving up a meeting with an arms dealer. Instead of me going to the team at Beale, the team is meeting me here in town." "This Foxtrot

Seven location?" I patted him on the cheek. "You're pretty smart for such a pretty face. Pops wants me to read you in. He has cleared it with your superior officers all the way up to Chief Hahn and the mayor. You are to pick two teams of five of the most trusted and skilled people. Can you drop me at 2200 Front Street and assemble your teams, then meet at this location for briefing in two hours?" "2200 Front Street, isn't that the car museum?" "Yeah, Poppy and Pops have been board members since it opened in 1983. I guess it played a significant role in why I'm such a Motorhead."

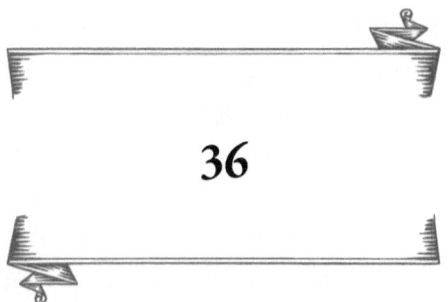

36

I WALKED INTO THE MUSEUM and was greeted by the curator with a warm smile, "Roxxanne Foxx" Mrs. Silva is a short, plump lady with grey hair and light blue eyes, so light they almost blend into the whites of her eyes. She has worked at the museum since its opening, starting as a receptionist. When we first met all those years ago, we instantly had a connection. As a young teenager, I was intrigued by this prim and proper lady who wrenched on cars and took a job at the car museum so that she could be around cars. Mrs. Silva and I had cars in common, but she initially took an interest in me when she found out I couldn't even drive yet but was starting college in the fall of that same year. Mrs. Silva hugged me tightly, "Hello, Dear, how are you?" Patting me on the cheek with her bear claws of hands that have never matched the rest of her typical grandma frame and demeanor. "I'm well, Mrs. Silva, are there people waiting for me in the basement?" "Yes, dear, but your Pops sent this package to you by messenger and wanted you to read your instructions before joining your personnel." She handed me a small box and a manila envelope. Pointing at the door off the main entrance to the museum, Mrs. Silva said, "Dear, please use my office to open your package. You will have privacy in there." Shutting the door, I said, "Thank you, Ma'am." I sat in one of the guest chairs across from Mrs. Silva's massive desk. I opened the plane manila envelope first. In it was an official letter with the White House seal on it. Attached to it was a handwritten note that read, "Red Roxx Foxx, the President insisted on reinstating you as Lt. Colonel. I can only advise him and explain that you retired as Captain and wouldn't take jumping in rank lightly. His statement was, and I quote, "This mission is too important to be carried out by a Captain." In the box, you will find an encrypted smartphone phone. It's time you joined the rest of the world. Love Pops" I opened the box to find a giant smartphone in a military-grade case. I whispered, "Shit!!" I turned on the phone and went to contacts with two numbers listed. Pops and Staff Sargent Craig Malone. I clicked Pops number, "Hello Sir, ok! Hi pops, Thank you for the note and explanation. Yes Sir, I understand. Standard orders? Yes Sir, Thank you, Sir, Hmm? Ok, Pops, I'll be careful. I love you too." I was hanging up the phone but still not thrilled with being reinstated two ranks above where I retired. As I usually do when wrapping my brain around something, I talked to myself while programming Connolly's number into the phone. "Really? Who does that? There is a ranking system for a reason. Seriously, who the hell does that? I know, a President, he does, that's who. Ok, Roxx, get your shit together." As I was about to stand to leave after my little talk with myself, a quiet wrap on the door, then Mrs. Silva said from the other side of the door, "Roxxanne dear, is it okay to enter?" "Yes, ma'am, it's all clear." She stuck her head in the partially opened door, "Dear, you have more people waiting for you. I directed them downstairs." "Thank you, Mrs. Silva. I'll be right there." I clicked on Connolly's number. "Hello," I said, "I guess Pops thought it was time for me to join the new millennium. He sent me an encrypted phone. You can save this number." Connolly chuckled. "It's about time! I got lucky it was a shift change at the house. I got one team together; the other I called in, and they are en route. Where are you?" "I'm upstairs in the curator's office. When I arrived, I was instructed to open a package from Pop before meeting with the team." "Well, you should probably get down here. That Craig guy from your house is wound a little tight. Oh, by the way, I heard from my buddy over in boat patrol they caught up to the Sundancer "Maggie," and he confirmed it's registered with the Coast Guard. It's Sam's boat. They located the boat tied up to a dock down in Clarksburg. Sam wasn't on board." "Ok, thank you, I'll be there in a minute." I walked out of Mrs. Silva's Office; she was at the reception desk working on a desktop computer. "Thank you for the use of your office. Why is it so quiet in here today?" "You are very welcome, dear. On special days like today, your Pops has me close the museum for maintenance." She winked one of her beautiful light blue eyes. "Ok, ma'am, if you need me, I'll be downstairs."

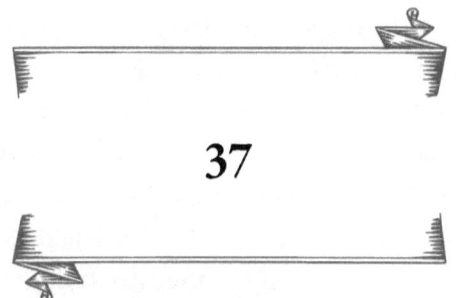

37

TEN-HUT, CRAIG ANNOUNCED. Fifteen or so men and women in black BDUs snapped to attention as I walked into the basement room. Looking around the room, I saluted, saying, "As you were" I looked over at Connolly and the Sac PD guys and crossed my eyes at him. He responded with a barely noticeable head shake. One of the PD guys elbowed Connolly in the ribs saying out the side of his mouth, "Dude, I bet she clanks when she walks!" I walked over to Connolly and his men and said, "Matter of fact, I do have brass balls, and they do clank when I walk." Connolly said, "Francis, did I mention Roxx has bionic-like hearing, you idiot." Francis said, "It's Frank, sorry Roxx, it's just, well, it's just Wow!" Connolly said, "Shut up, Francis!" I laughed, saying, "It's nice to meet you. I appreciate your help. Connolly, I have to speak with the Staff Sargent and get suited up. I'll be back for briefing in fifteen. There are drinks and snacks. Please help yourself." On cue, Craig appeared at my side with a stack of paperwork, blueprints, and photos. "Ma'am, I have your uniform waiting for you here. Here's your reading material." "Thank you, lead the way." I walked into the next room, once used as a janitor's closet or storage room. At the opposite side of the room from the door was a tri-fold partition. My BDUs draped over the top of the partition. Walking behind the partition, I said, "Go, Craig." He started his rapid fire of information at mock three. By the time I dressed, he had covered the basics of the subject and the mission. "Thank you. I will be out in a minute. Can you please send Detective Connolly in to see me?" "Yes, Ma'am" "Craig? When it's just the two of us, knock it off with the Ma'am crap." "Ok, Roxx, thanks.

It's bizarre after all the shit we have been through together. Have you heard from Sam?" "No, but Connolly's friend in boat patrol found his boat tied to a dock in Clarksburg, downriver about ten miles." "Humm, there's something in this communication stack with that word in it." "What word?" "Clarksburg, but I can't remember how or what's the significance." "Well, go find the information in that stack of crap, and on your way, send in Connolly." "10-4, on it!" Connolly swaggered into the janitor's closet, shutting the door behind him with a whistle, "Damn! You are hot." I smiled, sneaking a quick kiss before the briefing. "Pops and his boss thought it was a good idea to promote me to Lt. Colonel for reinstating me." "How long are you reinstated?" Using air quotes for reinstated. "You know, I didn't even think to ask, I assumed it was just for this mission, but I don't know." I was startled by a buzz in my ass, "What the hell!" I grabbed my back pocket, "I'm going to have to get used to this thing." Pulling out the smartphone from my back pocket. "It's a text from Craig, who is in the very next room. How dumb is that? Anyway, he has some more Intel for me." I felt like a dumbass texting Craig, "Get your Ars in here!" The door opened a second later. Craig shrugged. "Sorry, Roxx, I didn't want to interrupt you or anything." "What is it, Craig" "It's the word you said earlier, Clarksburg. It was in the chatter with an arms dealer named Juan Martinez. It's a meeting location." Connolly and I looked at each and, in unison, said, "Sugar Mill!" Craig said, "That was scary, don't do that again. There can't be two people who think like her." Connolly replied, "Don't worry, buddy, no one thinks like her, but we both know this area like the backs of our hands." Craig asked, "What is Sugar Mill?" I answered, "The Sugar Mill is just that. It's an old Sugar Mill." He said, "Oh, okay, I'll get on getting blueprints and get it up on the PowerPoint." I said, "Okay, good work Craig. Get the team studying it. We used to play "kick the can" there when I was a kid." Connolly said, "We played green witch there when I was a kid." Craig rolled his eyes in disgust and left us reminiscing. "I can't believe we never ran into each other. How old are you?" "Seriously, you don't ask a lady her age. How old are you?" "First, who's a lady? And second, I'm forty-five." Smacking his arm, "Whew! I'm younger than you by a few years. It never dawned on me to know your age."

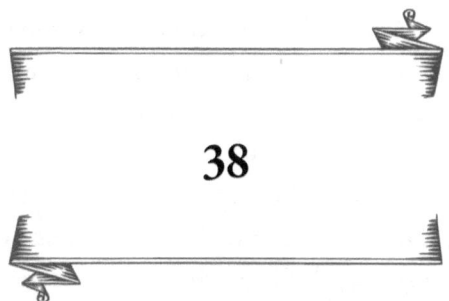

38

CONNOLLY AND I WALKED back into the room. Craig announced, "Ten Hut!" "The military personnel suddenly jumped to their feet, and the PD guys stiffened a little. "As you were!" Ely Stanlogovich's image was bigger than life on the giant screen. I asked Craig, "How old is that photo" "It was taken a month before Stanlogovich went underground about five years ago." "Is it the most recent photo you have?" "Yes, ma'am." "I need a computer." The airman closest to me jumped to his feet, "Ma'am!" I logged onto my encrypted email account and pulled up the email I sent to the crazy dentist's wife with the photos and the time-stamped video. I pulled up the headshot of the dentist and put it on the big screen next to the older photo of Stanlogovich. I logged out of my account and gave the airman his computer station back. "Airman, go through the video and put facial recognition to work on every person. While you are doing that, I want someone else to use the plate reader to read every license plate in the video, then cross-reference the faces with the plates." Two airmen said, "Ma'am, Yes, Ma'am!" I walked up to the big screen, looking at the two photos side by side. I said, "Shit! Connolly, are you seeing this?" "Yup, I sure am."

I stood at the front of the room to begin the briefing. Standing at the back of the room were five more men and women from Sac PD. "Good afternoon, ladies and gentlemen. My name is Lt. Colonel Roxxanne Foxx.

On the screen is Ely Stanlogovich. The photo on the left is from five years ago, before he came to our beautiful city and took the identity of Dr. Bryan Jones. DDS. The photos on the right are from last week. I took this photo in my civilian capacity as a Private Investigator, where he was the subject of infidelity surveillance. Subsequently, he was made aware of the surveillance. He has since made several attempts to neutralize the threat of revealing his identity.

Until a moment ago, we believed Ely Stanlogovich was at the head of this organization." Pointing at the tattoo in the older photo, "After closer review of the photo on the left, we now know he is the number two in the organization. On the upper chest and neck area, each Stanlogovich member wears a "suit." The tattoo shows their rank in the organization. On the crown of the snake is a number. Ely Stanlogovich has a number two. Ely's twin brother, the no-face Decedent, Igor Stanlogovich, was number three. Ivan Stanlogovich, the one-arm brother, is number four, and Bird face, Mikhail Stanlogovich, number five." Using a red marker, I put red marks across the face of each of the two dead brothers. I recited the details of how the two brothers ended up in the morgue and how Ivan was sporting a shiny prosthetic.

I continued with the briefing, pointing at the recent photo of Ely Stanlogovich, "As you can see the visible area of his upper chest and neck, he has significant scaring. One can presume he had the tattoos removed. He likely did so to take on his new identity and hide the prison ink from his wife, Mrs. Brenda Jones. Brenda Jones was my client for the infidelity investigation. Staff Sergeant, please put Mrs. Jones's photo up. Mrs. Jones is most likely the source for Ely finding out about the surveillance. Whether it was intentional or not, we don't know. In my last communication with Mrs. Jones, she was under duress when the phone call was disconnected. I believe she was trying to warn me about her husband. Now she is being held against her will by him along with Maggie Washington. Staff Sergeant, do you have a photo of Maggie?" "Yes, Ma'am, her California driver's license from three years ago." With a mouse click, Maggie's young face was on yet another screen. "Thank you, Staff Sergeant. Maggie Washington is the daughter of Samuel Washington; Sam is one of ours. Please put Sam's photo next to Maggie's. Maggie was abducted to use as leverage to get my location. With the car bomb and the news story leading people to believe Connolly and I perished, Maggie is no longer needed.

At this time, Sam is MIA, last seen heading south on the Sacramento River in his boat named Maggie. The Sacramento County Sheriff's boat patrol found it docked in Clarksburg."

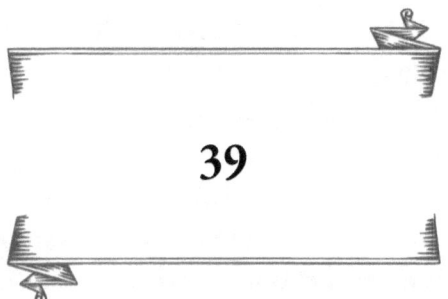

39

THE STANLOGOVICH SYNDICATE is considered a terrorist group. They are wanted in the killing and mutilation of an FBI agent, abduction and killing of a young girl, arms dealing, car bombing, kidnapping, human trafficking, drug dealing, and the list goes on.

Let's recap what we know, At least four members are related, and two of the four are deceased. Ely Stanlogovich is number two in the organization.

We also know a meeting with a known arms dealer in Clarksburg. An educated guess is it's at the Sugar Mill. As you are working on your task, airman, put it up on the two Screens over there." I pointed to the West side of the room. "Ma'am, yes, ma'am." "Connolly, can you have two teams of four? One team hit the house, and one hit the dentist's office? Coordinate to hit simultaneously. I want the rest of the team with us at the sugar mill, preferably people familiar with the area." A corn-fed-looking kid with strawberry blond hair and a beard said, "Excuse me, ma'am" I said, "Go, Ginger" He smiled a big smile that revealed a dip in his lower lip and said, "My daddy's orchard backs up to the "Sugar Mill" on the West side. I know that place like the back of my hand, including the underground rail system that runs out to the deep-water channel." "Staff Sergeant Malone, get on the horn with the Coast Guard, talk with Captain Han and have them get us a Helo and some boats on standby." As I gave orders to Sergeant Malone, I noticed Connolly and Ginger look at each other with unspoken communication. I continued, "What's the status of the blueprints for the sugar mill?"

"Ma'am, they should be here any minute." "While waiting, put the live satellite feed on that screen." Pointing at the East wall, "Ma'am, yes, ma'am!" With a click of the mouse, we were looking at the live satellite feed of the Sacramento River to the east, the Sugar Mill centered on the screen, and Sacramento deep water channel to the west. We studied the images fed to us from twenty-two thousand miles above the earth and to the South, somewhere near the equator. We all paused what we were doing except for the computers running face and license plate recognition when a polite Dong sounded. And the screens with Stanlogovich face plastered on them switched to CC feed triggered when anyone walks through the front door upstairs in the main lobby.

We watched as an airman walked to the reception desk and handed Mrs. Silva the cardboard tubes of blueprints. He said something and smartly turned around and walked back the way he came. Automatically the screen switches back to Stanlogovich face. I told the airmen closest to me, "Please go retrieve those from Mrs. Silva." "Ma'am, yes, ma'am!" I rolled my eyes and caught Connolly looking at me with those beautiful Brown bedroom eyes that seem to give him away whenever he thinks lustful thoughts. Smiling back at him, I said, "Connolly, can you introduce me to your people?" Without missing a beat, Connolly turned into his "Dan Aykroyd from Dragnet, Just the facts ma'am." He rattled off their names and position they hold at Sacramento PD, and their collateral assignments.

"This is Narcotics Detective Bob O'Sullivan, AKA "Ginger," he is also on SWAT. Detective Tam Hall, Vice, and SWAT. Detective Mike Brothers, Homicide and SWAT. Sergeant Bill Blake, Patrol Sergeant, and SWAT. Lieutenant Sandy Mills, Patrol Lieutenant, and SWAT. Captain Drew Hartman, Patrol, and SWAT. Detective Tom Smith, Narcotics and SWAT. Detective Betty O'Hare Homicide and SWAT. John Green, Patrol, and SWAT. I smiled and said to Connolly, "What did you do? Call in the entire SWAT team?' He said, "No, we have three SWAT teams. This is the day shift. They have days because they've been around the longest." I said, "Wow! Thank you for coming in to help us out. Are any of you snipers?" Ginger, Tam Hall, and Tim Smith all raised their hands. I nodded at them. They seemed to know I was a sniper. Being a sniper is like being part of a club.

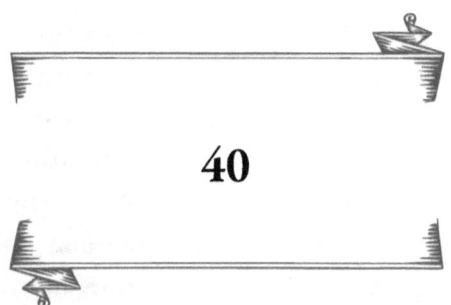

40

I TURNED MY ATTENTION to the airmen setting the blueprints up on a large, well-lit drafting table, using magnets to hold each corner of the blueprints. Lastly, he flipped a switch on the side of the table, turning on a light illuminating the blueprints from below. "Ginger, take a look and show us where the underground rail system is located." Ginger glanced at the blueprints and said, "It isn't on this set of blueprints." I shot a look at Staff Sergeant Malone. Craig said, "Ma'am, yes, ma'am, on it." Connolly smiled and said, "Craig, call the library on 10th street across from the Capital. Ask for Mrs. Connolly and tell her I need the original blueprints. Also, let her know Juanita will be by to pick them up in fifteen minutes." Connolly stepped away to call Juanita. He had his back on us as he talked to Juanita in Spanish. And was rolling his head with some ghetto attitude; we were all watching his back. Like we were watching a train wreck. He was still talking a mile a minute, and as he slowly turned around, he smiled, giving us a big shrug with his shoulders. He hung the phone up. "Juanita's pissed for interrupting his nail appointment, but he will be there in twenty minutes." I said, "Let's switch to the Dentist's office and the house in the Pocket. You guys decide who hits what, but I think the snipes will serve us better at the Sugar Mill." Captain Hartman spoke. "Team One, Lieutenant Mills, Sergeant Blake, and Officer Green, you take the dentist's office. Team Two, Detective O'Hare, and Brothers are with me at the Pocket house. Team Sugar Mill, O'Sullivan, Hall, and Smith, you are with Connolly and Lt. Colonel Foxx." I started to say thank you when the image of the receptionist caught my attention. I abruptly said, "Airman, freeze that frame, go back, stop, there!" Everyone focused on the image. I said, "It was well over a hundred degrees that day. Who wears a turtleneck sweater in the summer? sleeveless or not." Just as I was going to ask the airman what facial rec had to say about this lady? Several photos popped up on another screen. Some of which were from Interpol, Homeland Security, and the CIA. It was the beautiful receptionist from the dentist's office. Her hair was jet black instead of platinum blonde. She was wearing a sweat-stained wifebeater and black military fatigues. Across her chest from her breast and onto her neck was the suit tattoo. A human heart with an arrow through it, a snake wrapped around the arrow, the snake had a crown, on the first point of the crown was the number one. "Airman, please zoom in on that photo, concentrating on her left hip." As the airmen zoomed in, I saw she had a filet knife in a leather sheath on her hip. "Okay, people, we now know the head of the family. She is the number one suspect in the murder and mutilation of FBI Agent Jackson. I want to know everything about this person." I walked around the room, looking at all the photos as I spoke, retrieving information from every database in the world. It was rapid fire. The first airman said her name, "Haina Stanlogovich, date of birth October 1, 1972." Another airman said, "Birthplace, Odessa Russia, birth name meaning "Shiny Crown," served as a prison guard at IK14 prison in Mordovia, located in central Russia. Stanlogovich was terminated in 2013 when the federal penitentiary service deputy director ordered an investigation. During the investigation, a video surfaced of

Stanlogovich skinning a kitten alive to torment the prisoners. I glanced to the back of the room. The entire borrowed team was standing shoulder to shoulder, arms crossed their chests, soaking it all in every single detail as the rapid-fire kept going. "Interpol wants Haina Stanlogovich in connection with a bombing at a cafe in France killing six." I asked, "How long has she been in the US?" The airman said, "Unknown ma'am, she has been on a no-fly list since the bombing in France in 2014." I then asked, "When and where was the last known whereabouts?" another airman said, "Ma'am, 2014 when she released this video taking responsibility for the bombing." I said, "Go" The airman played the video on the largest screen at the front of the room. Haina Stanlogovich was centered in the video, with three of the brothers flanking her. Haina Stanlogovich was talking eerily calm about how the army of the Russian Crown would continue their mission until every Muslim was wiped off the face of the earth. I will take great pleasure skinning each and every one of them alive. I said, "I need Intel on the murdered FBI agent. Was he Muslim?" I heard clicking on the keyboards, but the answer came from the back of the room. Connolly said, "Yes, he was. I read it in the file our favorite FBI agent shared with me." Just then, the polite dong from the front door dinged, and the image of a portly Hispanic man sauntering in, wearing a pink silk scarf on his head tied under his chin with oversized white sunglasses on. He carried a tube under his arms and both hands out, palms facing down, trying not to smudge his fresh manicure.

I smiled and followed Connolly to the reception area. Connolly and Juanita's air-kissed each other like a couple of southern Belles, not wanting to mess with each other's lipstick. Connolly turned to me to introduce me; I stuck my hand out to shake Juanita's hand. Juanita said, "Oh please, girl." Then he gave me a big hug. I laughed and hugged Juanita back. I said, "Thank you for getting these for us." Juanita said, "Girl, anything for you. If you ever need anything, you just call." Then produced a black spam card with tiny little pink and purple hearts with "Juanita" in bold letters and a QR code. He said, "Just scan it, and it will call my private cell." Connolly was just standing there with a big goofy smile on his face. I said, "Thank you, Juanita." He hugged me again, turned to Connolly, and snapped his finger in a Z pattern. He turned on his heels, sashayed out the front door, got into a convertible BMW, and was off.

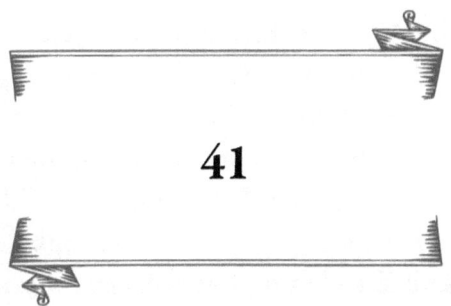

41

CONNOLLY AND I WERE heading to the door that led to the basement. Mrs. Silva said, "Roxxanne dear, your pops instructed me to retrieve this from the vault for you." Handing me a Pelican case made specifically for the long sniper rifle. I thanked her, bracing myself to lift the heavy case. I stumbled backward; the case was light as a feather. Mrs. Silva smiled and said, 'Careful, dear." I said, "Is there anything in this thing?" Shaking it with one hand. Mrs. Silva said, "Yes, dear, it is a prototype I built and sold to the military. Your pops were instrumental with the negotiations." I scoped it myself for up to 3000 yards with pinpoint accuracy. It is ready to go to work, dear." I was giddy with a new toy, but I caught myself. I don't think a Lieutenant Colonel would behave this way and cleared my throat and said in the most serious tone I could muster up, "Thank you, Mrs. Silva. I will take very good care of it and return it when the mission is complete." Mr. Silva said, "No, dear, I want you to have it." Like a little girl getting a new pink Barbie Jeep, I jumped up and down and said, "Yay!" and hugged Mrs. Silva. I caught myself again and looked around the room. Connolly was standing in the downstairs doorway, chuckling at me as I straightened my BDUs. As I approached him, he said. "You might want to contain that big smile, killer." The three snipers noticed the long Pelican case when we walked into the command room. Then eyebrows raised, no other movement except a slight twinkle in their eyes. Then Ginger winked as in the confirmation of what they already had suspected. My hip vibrated. I took my old school pager off my waistband; it was the number the hospital security guard gave us of the

Uber driver Sam called. Then another page with 911. I called the number; Goth's voice wasn't the laid back. I'm too cool to talk to you voice from earlier. Goth was shouting hyper speed. She said, "I'm sorry I didn't tell you the whole truth earlier, but I didn't know if I could trust you. I'm still not sure. I mean, I don't know if I do or can trust you now, but I think I can. You seem like you are nice, well, Sam and Maggie and I are friends, and I'm, I'm, I don't know, I don't know what to do." I said, "Goth, slow down. It's okay. Start from the beginning." Goth took a big breath and said, "I'm friends with Sam and Maggie. I live near them at the river. Sam watches out for me. So, I picked him up when he called earlier and needed help. After I dropped him off at the Marina, I was so worried. I've been hanging out. You know near where you talked to me earlier?" I said, "Yes, go on." Goth started talking hyper-speed again. "I was waiting at the Marina, and this big gold four-door Mercedes drives in and parks right next to me. The driver looked over at me, and his eyes, they looked, they looked dead. This evil-looking, skinny chick was in the passenger seat with short blond hair. And in the back seat was this giant freak with one arm. The evil bitch said something, but I couldn't hear her. Then the freak in the back seat yanked Maggie and another lady out of the car. Maggie looked right at me. She looked terrified." "Goth, what did the other lady with Maggie look like?" Goth said, "She looked like a snooty housewife in designer clothes, but she looked terrified too. After they entered the gate, I snuck over to see which dock they went to and what their boat looked like. It was one of those big pee pee boats." I said, "Pee pee boat?" She said, "Yeah, you know, Like one of those long speedboats, middle-aged guys get to overcompensate for a small pee, pee." I smiled, trying not to laugh, and asked, "Did you see a name or a number on the boat?" She said, "No, but you can't miss it. It's really long with a pickle fork bow. It was all white with a big bright gold Crown towards the back." "Could you see if they went upriver or downriver?" "No, but I could hear them. They went downriver." I said, "This is great, Intel Goth. Do you know where the car museum is on 3rd street?" Goth said, "Yes" "Can you please come here? I will meet you in the front lobby." "Yes, I'll be there in five minutes" After she hung up, I relayed the information to the room. "Staff Sergeant, get ahold of the Coast Guard, get them moved but do not approach. Just observe and report. Drop some names if you have to." Craig responded with, "Ma'am, yes, ma'am" "Connolly, can you get your Sheriff friends on standby? That boat is fast enough to dust most of the LEO boats, but we could outnumber them and cut them off before they get to open water." Without a word, Connolly calmly started making calls. I went upstairs to speak with Mrs. Silva. I explained to her the situation with Goth and told her I think Goth is a special girl. I asked, "Can Goth hang out with her until the mission is complete?" Mrs. Silva said, "Of course, dear, I would be glad to keep a certain young lady company. You know it wasn't so terribly long ago when I kept company with another special young lady?" I said, "Thank you, Mrs. Silva, but sometimes it feels like a hundred years ago." Goth walked in almost at a stagger, falling into my arms. She had a knife wound to the left side of her abdomen. I yelled, "Call

911" Then I heard what sounded like a herd of elephants coming up the stairs. I was applying pressure to the wound when Connolly and the team ran through the doors from the basement. Connolly and Ginger stopped to help me with Goth. The rest of the team went outside to clear the parking lot. Goth whispered, "The evil bitch caught me looking in the window of the Mercedes and attacked me. She was screaming in some strange foreign language. She didn't follow me. She left before me, and I saw her going down Broadway towards the Tower Café." The ambulance arrived and started working on the semi-unconscious Goth. "Ginger, can you please see if you can find her identification? They will need her full name at the hospital. The Prius outside is hers. Mrs. Silva, would you mind going with Goth to the hospital? I need to get to work on this mission." "Mrs. Silva said, "Of course, dear, I will stay with her until you finish the mission." She leaned in and quietly said, "Dear put them down." I said, "Yes, Ma'am." Goth started flopping around, and one of the medics started rattling orders to another medic. "She's going into shock!" Then the other medic said, "She has a medical ID bracelet. She's Diabetic" They juiced her with glucose and bolted to the awaiting ambulance. Ginger handed Mrs. Silva Goth's driver's license as she was scrambling into the back of the ambulance with one of the attending medics and were off with sirens blaring in the direction of UC Davis. "Connolly, can you get a couple of unmarked cars to keep an eye on this place." He said, "Yeah, and I have people at the scene of the attack." I said, "Goth described the car as a gold four-door Mercedes."

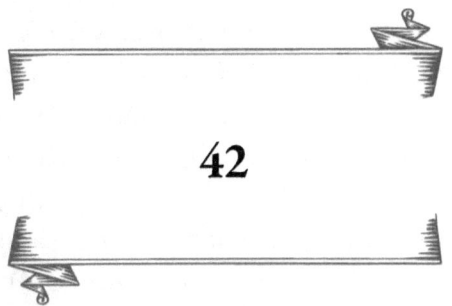

42

WE BROKE UP INTO THREE teams. Each team leader briefed the teams on their position and each team member's objective. The pocket house team leader had the room first. Detective O'Hare had the slightest Irish brogue that reminded me of my mother. It was beautiful. I could listen to her all day long. My mind wandered, thinking of my mother. I tuned back in as team leader O'Hare said, "Captain Hartman, you and Airman Freeman take a position here and here." Pointing at the front of the property at each corner. She clicked the mouse to Google Street View. "You can cover the front and along each side of the house from these positions. Brothers, you are with me at the back of the house. We will gain access from the back neighbor's fence; it appears to be a six-foot block wall." One of the other SWAT members popped off, "So O'Hare, that means you will scale the fence, not go through it like that last time." All the SWAT members started laughing, including O'Hare. O'Hare retorted, "The "Melter" didn't get away, did he?" I giggled at the term "Melter" Poppy used to use when one of his construction guys was annoying him. Team Dentist had the room next; Officer Green had the aerial view of the dentist's office on the screen. He pointed at each access point, assigned the members to each location, and then switched to Street View. As soon as I saw the office door, it all fell into place. It hit me like a ton of bricks. The dentist's office door was a large ornate red door. I replayed the surveillance from the beginning and fast forward. I saw dozens of so-called patients going in and out of there. I started talking to myself, unaware I wasn't using my inside voice. "Roxx, you are a complete, total feckin eejit. How did you miss that?" O'Hare raised an eyebrow at my self-punishing outburst. Connolly said, "What's up, Roxx?" I snapped too, and I looked around the room and said, "Well, it's a good thing I don't get embarrassed because this would be one of those times."

I debriefed the teams about recovering a girl named Susie from human trafficking. I explained I had help from an older prostitute named Shelby. The human traffickers posted Susie's photo on a dating site, using air quotes called "Red Door." I ran into the old prostitute, Shelby, on the street near Tower Café." I pointed to the spot on the map. "Connolly and I were at the crime scene where the attack on Sam and Maggie happened." I pointed to the map again. "I stood here, talking to Shelby. I felt like someone was watching us. The dentist's office appeared entirely abandoned. Despite her fear of the men behind the red door, Shelby was instrumental in getting Susie out. That is what Shelby called them. After seeing the dentist's front door and remembering all the foot traffic at the dentist's office, I believe the dentist's office is their headquarters.

Ginger, you know the ins and outs of the Sugar Mill. You should be the team leader."

Ginger said, "Yes, ma'am" Connolly's phone started ringing, and he stepped back to take a call. Approximately fifteen seconds later, staff Sergeant Malone's phone started ringing. They both hung up, and both started talking at the same time. They reported that the white offshore jet boat turned into Whiskey Slough heading towards the deep-water channel.

I said, "Ginger, we better make it quick, or we will be late to the party."

Ginger had the plot map with the underground rail on it up on a bulletin board and the Sugar Mill blueprints next to it on another bulletin board. He said, "The rail goes into a tunnel here. They built it to be functional at low tide or high tide with split-level rails. When it's low tide, it comes out at this point and this level of the dock. When it's high tide, it comes out at this level of the dock. Just by switching the track inside the tunnel right here." Pointing at the plot map.

I interrupted, "Staff Sergeant, what is the tide schedule?" "Ma'am, high tide will peak in fifteen minutes, then it will be slack tide, and then the rush will be on. Luckily the deep-water channel is a dead end at the harbor. It doesn't have the flow like the river when the tide goes out. The rush isn't that bad."

Ginger continued laying out the operation. "I want a sniper here." Pointing at the levee across the deep-water channel from the tunnel's mouth. Coast Guard will be stationed here and here." Pointing at the map of the deep-water channel just North of the tunnel around a small bend. I suggested the second Coast Guard boat should be stationed just South of Whiskey Slough, tucked into Miner Slough. Most likely, the arms dealer they are meeting with will be coming up the deep-water channel from the Bay. "Affirm, Ma'am," said Staff Sargent Malone. "That was the chatter we've heard." Ginger continued switching gears to the old Sugar Mill grounds. "The Sugar Mill was recently converted to an entertainment venue with an outdoor stage." Pointing to the East side of the property. "I want a snipe on top of the stage structure to cover the East side of the main building and the loading dock. I want another snipe on the roof of the mill elevator to cover the loading dock and towards the deep water channel. The ground crew can use my old pickup to go to daddy's orchard and approach from here and here. Y'all in the tunnel, it's pitch black in there, so you'll need your night vision. You come up here at the bottom of the mill elevator. There's a catwalk here, so watch your cover overhead too."

Staff Sergeant Malone said, "Ma'am, I just received a message. The chatter says the meet is at 2200 hours, and some kind of exchange is going down. The inside guy said, G-4G." "As in the letter G?" "Ma'am, yes, ma'am." I looked at my watch. It gives us four hours. I started to say we better gear up when another alarm bell went off. The main screen switched from the satellite feed to the loading bay. It was a military transport. I glanced at staff Sergeant Malone. "Ma'am, yes, ma'am, Airmen Freeman, you are with me."

I was watching the transport truck when my phone rang. I didn't recognize the number, but it was a 916-area code. I answered it with some suspicion in my tone. Mrs. silva's voice said, "Dear, it's me, Mrs. Silva." "Hello, ma'am. How is Goth?" "Britney, Britney Ames, dear. She's still in surgery and probably will survive, but she can lose her left kidney. Here comes the doctor. I'm Britney's mother, so I must go, but I will call you back. Goodbye, dear." I continued watching the loading bay. There were three airmen from the truck, plus Craig and Airmen Freeman.

They unloaded the truck with gear, guns, ammo, and food. They offloaded platters and platters of food.

My phone rang again from the same* 916-number. I answered,

"Hello, ma'am" "Hello dear, I am calling with some good news." With some relief in her voice. "Britney will recover fully, and the doctor saved her kidney." I exclaimed, "That is great news!" As I continue watching the truck. "Thank you, ma'am," And hung up. As soon as I did, pop called. "Hello, Pops. I'm standing here watching the loading bay. I presume this was you're doing?" "Well, you know the military motto? Eat when you can." I laughed, "Yes, Sir, also, I received the gift from Mrs. Silva. I haven't even had the chance to open the case yet." "You are going to love it. Mrs. Silva is an engineering genius and a very wealthy one too. "If I know Mrs. Silva, She could care less about the dough. It's more about the build." "You probably know her better than anyone. And she built one hell of a riffle. I have never seen anything like it. If you noticed, it's extremely light. She developed a combination of lightweight metal, using Titanium for strength and carbon fiber alloy for the components. Additionally, she developed a 308 caliber round that is water resistant." I briefed Pop on the status of the operation." Pop said, "You better get some of that food. It's going to be a long night." "Yes, Sir,

thank you, Sir," Pop wished me luck, and we said our goodbyes.

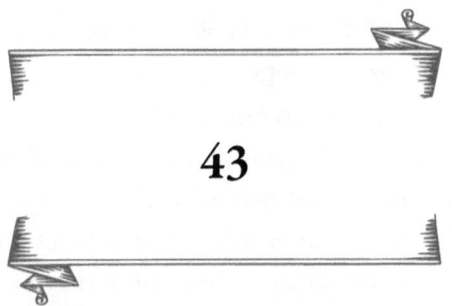

43

HAINA STANLOGOVICH walked into one of the flop houses on Y St, slamming the door behind her. Two of the handlers jumped to attention. They both were wearing black short sleeve t-shirts and black pants. Both men had shaved heads and were covered with prison gang tattoos. Twenty girls were lying on filthy mattresses on the floor in the front room and the adjoining room that once was used as the dining room. Haina Stanlogovich said, "Soberi vsekh devushek is drugikh mest O prevdi ikh syuda- *Get all the girls from all the other locations and bring them here.*"

Without saying a word, both men walked to the front door to follow their orders. When they got in the limo bus, one man said to the other, "Eta suka sumasshedshaya- *That bitch is crazy*" The other man simply said, "Da-*Yes*." Pulling off the curb to complete their orders. Haina Stanlogovich kicked one of the girls lying on the floor and screamed, "Slight yoga hor" Another man dressed much like the other two men, except his shirt was a black long-sleeve dress shirt. His head was also shaved, but all his ink was below the shirt's collar.

Watching Haina in this state was arousing him. He had never met any woman with his sadistic nature until he met Haina. He had noticed the blood on the sheath of Haina's knife. The thought of her plunging her knife into flesh gave him an erection. Haina knew what he was thinking. She caught him staring at her knife. She licked her lips as she walked over to him. She rubbed his crotch as she passed him, walking to the backroom. The backroom was off-limits to everyone except Haina and Viktor. Viktor followed Haina into the room. As he shut the door, she lunged at Viktor. She ripped at his shirt, buttons flying everywhere. He slammed her against the wall, leaving an impression on the drywall. He grabbed her knife from the sheath on her hip. The razor-sharp knife sliced through her sweater like butter, revealing her large breasts. He nicked her at the base of her neck, and a small trickle of blood ran down her neck, arousing him even more. He sucked the blood, lifting her against the wall. She wrapped her strong legs around his waist, sliding down onto him. As he was pumping in and out, in and out, he was slamming her against the wall. The closer they got to cumming, he slammed her harder and harder against the wall. Haina was choking him, cutting off his airflow, his eyes rolling to the back of his head as they both came. She screamed, "Boleh boleh- *more, more*" Some people kiss each other intimately after sex. Haina backhanded Viktor then licked the blood from his busted lip. She looked him in the eyes, saying, "Razbudi devshek- *wake the girls.*" Viktor let go of his grasp on Haina and grabbed an identical shirt on his way out the door to replace the one Haina had destroyed.

He went to the dingy kitchen to prepare the hot shot. Haina dressed in black military pants and a black wife beater much too small for her, barely covering her large breasts and exposing her entire suit. It was her official business attire. Looking in the mirror, she smiled at the nick on her neck and said a little closer to the right, and Viktor would have been fucking a corpse. She swiped the blood and licked her finger, getting wet all over again. Still smelling of sweaty sex, she sniffed each of her armpits. She smiled at the musky odor and thought the spicks might like it. Viktor was in the dank kitchen heating the crank to a liquid form on a large piece of aluminum foil. Each side of the foil rolled up so it wouldn't spill once it was in liquid form. He used two syringes to suck up all the liquid meth, enough hotshot for the twenty girls. Viktor shoots the first half of the girls with the first syringe and the other half of the girls with the second syringe. Each hot shot is ten units, enough to wake the girls without them tweaking too hard. Viktor knows to give them just enough to make them want more and to do whatever or whoever for their next fix. He also knows that if they tweak too hard and they'll become unruly, he will have to give them a hit of "H" to sedate them, and heroin is more expensive than meth.

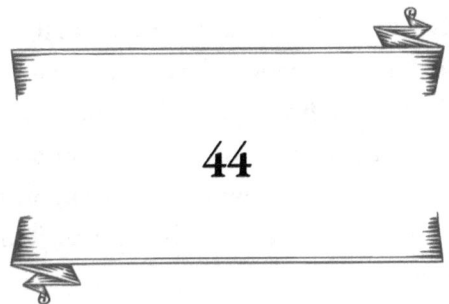

44

ROXXY WAS STANDING at the table set up for the food trays. She had a large paper plate in her hand, piling the cold cuts, cheese, fresh veggies, and spinach dip, avoiding the bread and chips, not wanting to go into a carb coma right before the mission. Connolly sidled up next to Roxxy, snitching a piece of cheese off her plate. "So, have you peeked at it yet?"

I looked at him sideways with a big grin. "No, I've been waiting, so we could peek at it together."

"Well, alright, let's go peek at it together." "Follow me." "With pleasure."

I giggled and said, "You always say that." "Because it's always true."

Roxxy grabbed the plate of food and the long Pelican case. They went to the room that was once a janitor's closet, now a dressing room. Roxxy set her plate down on the edge of a utility sink and found a stack of paper towel boxes to use as a table. She unsnapped the case, opened it just a little, peeked through the crack, and then slammed it shut. "Okay, I peeked."

Connolly laughed, "Oh man! That's just mean."

Laughing out loud, saying, "I know, right." Opening the case all the way, they just stood there looking at it. It was magnificent. It was like a piece of art in a gallery. Literally, it was even signed and numbered by Mrs. Silva, number 001.

Connolly said, "It looks like a sexy version of the Remington M24."

"It's like the skinny sister to the Remington M 2010. A cross between the Remington M 2010 or a really fat sister of a Barrett M 107 with a detachable magazine box. With a Titans suppressor."

Connolly lifted it out of the case, "Woo, I think I might have creamed a little"

"Right, it's not the thirty pounds like the Barrett, is it?" Popping a cube of cheese in my mouth. "Lean against that door, I have to gear up, and there isn't a lock on it."

He leaned against the door with arms crossed over his chest and legs crossed at his ankles. He was watching with a Cheshire grin across his gorgeous face. I dropped the BDUs to the floor. Then I unbuttoned my shirt. I was buckass naked. I picked up my ultralightweight wet suit. Connolly started to come over to me but stopped in his tracks when there was a wrap on the door.

I scooped up the BDUs and the wet suit and jumped behind the partition. I yelled, "Enter" "Ma'am, I just received a message from the Whitehouse. The President wants a zoom call with you and the team in fifteen minutes." "Shit, why?"

"The message said the President wants to fill you in on why he has taken an active role in this mission." "Okay, get everyone briefed. I'll be out in five." "Ma'am, yes, ma'am."

I heard the door shut and a thrump sound of Connolly leaning against the door again. I came out from behind the partition struggling with the wet suit. Trying to get any wet suit over the shoulders is a bitch, ultralightweight or not. I walked to Connolly, "Can you give me a hand with this?" Connolly bent over, saying, "I rather not." he kissed my nipple, one then the other. "Oh my God." Smiling, he spun me around and helped me get the suit over my shoulders.

He spun me around again, facing him, kissing me long and deep. He bent down for the zipper, pulling just above my right knee. As he zipped up the suit, he stopped at my hip slipping his hand inside my suit.

Another rap on the door with a muffled voice saying, "Five minutes, ma'am." I sighed and zipped my suit up the rest of the way. I scrambled into my BDUs and out the door.

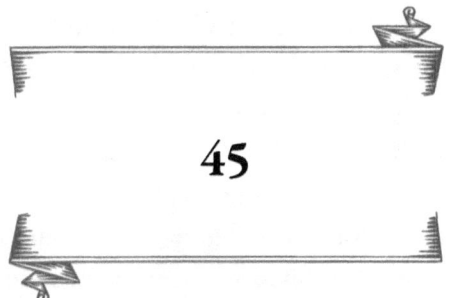

45

THE BORROWED SACRAMENTO Police Department team, the airmen, and I were standing at attention in front of the screen with the presidential seal on it. The screen flickered. In a flash, The President of the United States was standing at a podium. The presidential seal is in the background. The American flags were on either side of him. The airmen and I saluted the commander-in-chief. The President said, "At ease, Lieutenant Colonel Foxx. Your Pops advised me," We heard someone off camera clear their throat. The President looked in the direction of the sound, irritated. The President said, "Damn it, John, it is what it is, it's a small team, and I don't think any of them except for you and Lieutenant Colonel Foxx will give a hoot that you are her Pops. The two of you work for me." I felt about fifty eyes on the back of my head. "As I was saying, Lieutenant Colonel Foxx, John briefed me on the mission. I want to take this opportunity to personally thank you for taking this mission on." He picked up a two-inch-thick book and plunked it down on the podium. "Lieutenant Colonel Foxx, do you know what this is?" "Sir, no Sir" "This is you; this is from when you were recruited. It's from when you were just a little girl going to college. Much, much younger than your peers at the time, and it's your service record. It's every operation you were ever on." He continued, with his hand on the book. "This is why I know you were the perfect choice to lead this mission. You know of the FBI agent killed, deboned, and mailed back to us?" "Sir, yes, Sir." His voice was a little quieter, a little softer. "He was much like you in many ways. He, too, went off to college much younger than his peers. He was my best friend's only son and my God son. Lieutenant Colonel, your standing orders are in effect. You get them sumbitches by any means, Godspeed." The screen went black. I slowly turned around to face the twenty-five or so men and women. Not sure what I would read on their faces or in their eyes. Within every set of eyes, I saw tears. I saw pride. I saw respect. I saw sister and brotherhood. It was a different type of mission pep talk but the most effective one I have ever heard. I didn't doubt we would have each other's six on the mission, but now I know we will forever be bonded.

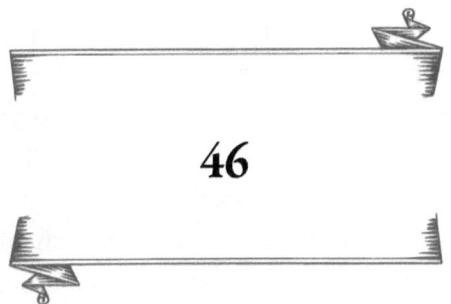

46

QUIETLY STANDING IN front of the team, looking at each one and remembering every detail of their faces. Every crease, every line, reading their eyes, suddenly we all jumped to the sound of Zzz zzz.

I said, "Excuse me," Taking the pager off my hip, slightly annoyed with the interruption, until I saw the number and the code. I didn't recognize the phone number, but it was the code I gave Shelby for emergencies when she helped me recover Susie. Dialing the number, I was worried the Russians somehow figured out Shelby helped me. Shelby answered tower café. I sighed in relief. I said, "Are you okay? What's going on?" In a professional voice. She said, "Please hold, ma'am. I'll check on your order." And placing me on hold. A couple of seconds later, she was back on the line.

In the background, I could hear pots and pans banging around. A man's voice with a strong Greek accent says, "Pick up five tops." A little bell was dinging. Shelby said, "Sorry for all the noise. I'm in the kitchen. Something is going down on, on the street. The girls I help started the night shift about an hour ago, and the men behind the red door are scooping them up and forcing them into a big party bus. You know, like the ones the casinos use." I asked, "How do you know something is about to go down?" "I was out back having a cig, and one of the men yanked a girl out of her date's car right in the middle of a date. Then pointed a gun at the date. The car was nice, and they don't want regular people to know who they are, and now they don't care who sees them." I asked, 'When do you get off work?"

She said, "I get off at 11:00." "Good, you stay there and stay inside the restaurant.

I'm on this, do you understand me? Shelby, I need to do this without worrying about you, too, so please stay inside. You can keep an eye on Broadway through the windows, but please stay inside." Shelby said, "Okay." She raised her voice a little and said, "Yes, ma'am, you could pick up the to-go orders at the front reception desk," I clicked the end button on the phone's screen and put it in my back pocket. I said, "To the team, we need to get in position. They're on the move. Team dentist office, they are in a party bus in your area, scooping up the girls." Three black sprinter vans and an old beat-up Ford ranch truck backed into the loading bay.

Ginger said, "Your Chariots await." We all loaded each team in a sprinter van. En route, we all were handed earbuds. I asked, "Are they waterproof?" Ginger said, "Yes, ma'am." I asked, "Do you have a small dry bag for my pager and phone?" He smiled a big goofy smile with a big dip of chew in his lower lip, handing me a small dry bag with a strap that looked like a fanny pack. "Seriously? A fanny pack? Do I look that old?" Laughing, "You're almost old enough for me to date." and winked. Connolly said, "Ginger, are you hitting on my girl?" The corn-fed kid puffed up his chest and said, "What if I am, old man?" Connolly puffed up his chest, "I might be able to take you if I hit you over the head with my walker." Ginger laughed and blew Connolly an air kiss. The sprinter van pulled to the shoulder of the levee road, about a half mile North of the tunnel opening. I opened the side door of the sprinter van, strapping the waterproof rifle drag bag to my back. I asked, "Who will cover my tab at O'Doul's if I make it a cross in one breath?" Staff Sergeant Malone said over his shoulder from the driver's seat, "Don't take that bet. It's a setup. She swims like a fish and drinks like one too." "Shut up, Craig, you party pooper." I slammed the door the van pulled off the shoulder as I took a deep breath to go under the water.

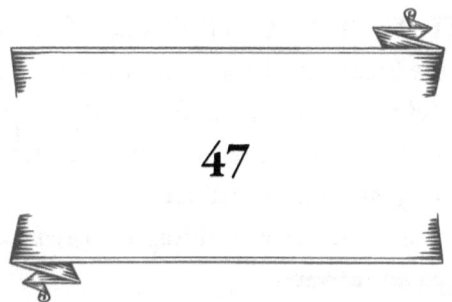

47

I MADE IT TO THE OTHER side of the deep-water channel in one breath. As I was swimming across, I thought of my dad. Before my mom and dad died, dad and I would swim for hours—competing with who could hold their breath the longest. Dad would let me win every once in a while. Dad was a master at holding his breath, swimming countless laps underwater.

I scrambled up the levee bank and took my BDUs and boots out of the drag bag. I slipped out of my wet suit and swim shoes. I put my BDUs and boots on. I stashed my wet suit and swim shoes in the side pocket of the drag bag. I swung the bag over my shoulder. I jogged the half mile or so to a location directly across the deep-water channel from the tunnel. I fully opened the drag bag to use it as a shooting mat. I laid on my stomach and unfolded the legs of the bipod. I inserted a magazine box loaded with ten rounds. On the mat were two more identical magazine boxes. I flipped up the lens covers and scoped the tunnel and pier. As I watched Team Sugar Mill get in position, I heard Team Dentist and Team Pocket check in.

They were in place and had a thirty-second countdown. "Team Pocket House, team leader O'Hare, check, in position." "Hartman, check, in position." "Freeman, check, in position." "Brothers, check-in position." "Team Dentist, Green, check, in position." "Mills, check, in position." "Sanders, check, in position." "Blake, check, in position." O'Hare counted down, "Five, four, three, two, one- Execute operation breach!"

Next, I heard the loud door rams, glass breaking, and the officers announcing themselves. "Sacramento PD, search warrant" Then different team members, said, "Clear, clear, all clear. Both team leaders announced both locations were deserted. Connolly's voice appeared on the radio. "O'Hare, release the scene to patrol and get CSI on both locations. Both teams get to the Sugar Mill. Approach from the O'Sullivan farm." "Copy!"

Staff Sargent Malone was talking in my ear, "Lt. Colonel, I just got an update." "Go ahead." "There are two Formula 500's running up the deep-water channel." "Say again, did you say two Formula 500s?" "Ma'am, that is affirm!" Those boats have quad V12s, each motor running about six hundred horses." "Ma'am, yes, ma'am."

"Team Sugar Mill, Ginger, check, in position." "Hall, check, in position." "Smith, check, in position." "Connolly, check, in position." "Foxx, check, in position."

The pocket house team and Dentist team arrived at the O'Sullivan farm. They were approaching the Sugar Mill on foot through the orchard. Each team member is in every other row of almond trees. Ginger said to the two teams, "Hold your positions in the trees, be ready to move." "Copy that."

I said, "I spy with my little eye, a white pickle fork jet boat with a gold crown on the side." The boat idled at the pier. "Two male subjects and two female friendlies. The females are Maggie Washington and Brenda Johnson."

Connolly's voice whispered, "I have eyes on Sam. He is on the overhead conveyor belt, moving towards the inner tunnel opening." "Remember, team; Sam is friendly." "Copy,"

Ely told One-arm, "Stay with the boat and direct the Mexicans inside." "Da, *Yes,*" said One-arm.

Ginger said, "Two vehicles are approaching from the east. No, make that three. A sedan, a limo bus, and what appears to be a decommissioned U-Haul moving truck,"

Off in the distance, I can hear the fast boats approaching and throttling down. The deep-water channel is a dead end because the locks are broken in the closed position. And many years of silt built up on the riverside, the outgoing tide is slightly noticeable. The large fifty-foot boats didn't need much more than an idle to maneuver up the channel to the pier. Each boat docked at the pier. One-arm pointed to the tunnel with his shiny hook.

Connolly's voice whispered, "Ely, Maggie, and Brenda are inside the plant." Maggie was dragging her feet and struggling to get away from Ely. "The arms dealers are in the plant now. "Maggie is loose and running back through the tunnel."

Using a Nextel, Ely ordered Ivan, "Kill that little bitch when she gets to the pier." "Da, *Yes*" One-arm stood directly in front of the tunnel. He cocked his head to one side as if he was listening to something. He removed a large knife from a sheath at the small of his back and stepped to one side of the tunnel.

Maggie was running full speed towards the mouth of the tunnel. Her legs were getting heavy, her breath was labored, and the back of her throat was dry and burning. She was almost free from the nightmare. Something stopped her in her tracks. Someone grabbed her from behind. She let out a muffled scream but was relieved it was Sam. Sam shushed her, whispering, "Slow down. You don't know what is waiting for you out there." Maggie's eye's widened with fear. She looked back into the tunnel, weighing her options. Sam took her by the hand, walking towards the mouth of the tunnel. They were hugging the wall of the tunnel. As Sam and Maggie exited the tunnel, One-arm lunged from his hiding spot, knife out front of him. "Pfft, pfft" One-arm crumpled to the ground like a bag of dirty laundry. Sam covered Maggie, looking across the channel. He couldn't see me but raised his hand in a wave. He took Maggie by the hand, and they scrambled up the riprap of the levee bank, heading north along the channel.

I said, "One-arm is down. Sam and Maggie are on foot, heading north on the levee. Staff Sargent, have boat patrol to tow the boats off the pier. Team Pocket, make your way to the deep water channel on the north side of the mill to the tunnel opening. Flank the tunnel." I heard, "Ma'am, yes, ma'am." First from Staff Sgt. And then "Copy" from O'Hare.

The U-Haul truck backed up to the loading dock of the mill. The limo bus with the drugged girls nosed up to the dock next to the U-Haul. Viktor parked the Mercedes next to the limo bus. Haina and Viktor got out of the car, and the two-armed men from the bus followed suit. Ely was waiting for Haina and Viktor at the top of the concrete stairs of the loading dock. The man from the U-Haul exited the truck. Staff Sgt. Malone said, "The U-Haul driver is the under-cover ATF." "Maptnhec haxoantcr BHyTph (Martinez is inside)" Ely said. The group walked through the large bay door. Haina tossed her chin in Brenda's direction and said, "no4eny 3ta tynar cyka 3n ecb n3baBntbcr o *thee, Why is that stupid bitch here? Get rid of her.*" "Da, *Yes*" Ely produced a blade from across his lower back. Brenda started to plead with Ely, "Bryan, don't do this, please. I love you. Please don't do this." Streams of black mascara ran down Brenda's face. "You stupid cow, shut up." He grabbed Brenda by the elbow and dragged her from the shadow of the bay door. "I have a shot," said Ginger. "Take it" Ely raised his hand to cut Brenda's throat with a backhand slash. "Pfft, pfft," double tap to the head. Martinez and the other boat driver ran for the tunnel. "Martinez and crew are running for it, Roxx." "Copy, Coast Guard helo, just picked me up. We are waiting for them." All hell broke loose in the old Sugar Mill. Connolly, the undercover ATF, and the airmen surrounded the two limo drivers. "Freeze, Sac PD, don't move." "ATF, don't fucking move." Haina and Viktor ran for the Mercedes, leaping from the loading dock. "Pfft, pfft, pfft, pfft." Two snipers, two shots each, one in the head, one through the ribs into the heart. They were dead before they hit the ground. Like two birds with broken wings, it wasn't a soft landing. The two Russian men smiled at Haina's demise as they raised their hands straight into the air.

Martinez and his Amigo ran out of the tunnel. Skidding to a stop as the helo flipped the searchlights on. I was hanging out the open door on the helo skids. My new shiny rifle had Martinez in its crosshairs. And the gunny had the amigo in his. The pilot said, "United States Coast Guard, freeze." Martinez started to raise his weapon. "Pfft," one to the head. He looked bewildered as he remained standing for a split second. Then his lifeless body crumpled where he once stood.

The wiser amigo dropped his gun and raised his hands into the night air. Team Pocket approached from both sides of the tunnel. O'Hare was commanding the amigo, "Put your hands on your head, interlace your fingers, get down on your knees. With each command, there was a repeat in Spanish by Brothers. "*Pont us manos en tu cabeza, encaje interior tus dedos ponte de rodillas.*"

O'Hare gave us a thumbs up and escorted the amigo back through the tunnel.

"Captain, can you please drop me off on the south side of the Sugar Mill." "10-4" A few minutes later, I thanked the captain for the lift. The helo was off the McClellan Air Base.

NEXT FRIDAY

Sam's Sundancer was anchored in the five-mile-an-hour zone across from Old Sacramento. Jack was on the boat's bow in a skimpy bikini, waving at us as we idled up to them. Connolly tied fenders to the stainless cleat of the new 520 Sundancer. I idled "The Poppy" slightly past "The Maggie" to slide down next to her. Connolly tossed a line to Sam on the bow of "The Maggie." At the stern, O'Hare tossed Maggie a line. Sam walked down the gun well to show Maggie how to tie the line to the cleat.

As 'The Poppy" and "The Maggie" rafted up in the Sacramento River, the sun went down, and the city's lights started to twinkle. I said, "Can I have your attention?" I raised my beer into the air. The team raised their drink in unison. I continued, "Other than Jack, Sam, and Maggie, I have been an only child. Looking at you all today, my family has grown. Here's to Family, Cheers!"

THE END

MICHELLE WISHART

TURN THE PAGE EXCERPT

Please note the following sneak peek is a work in progress and may have some artistic changes at the time of publication.

The first in the John Hunt series, retired EDSO Captain John Hunt finds himself involved in a dangerous case against the ruthless Neo Nazi splinter cell of "The Order" called "The New World Order" involving Human Trafficking, Drug running and Revenge.

HUMAN
CARGO

MICHELLE WISHART

1984

In 1984 "The Order" reared its ugly head. The Order was a white supremacist terrorist group founded by Robert Mathews. Mathews, a baptized Mormon, formed the terrorist group of predominantly Mormon Survivalist. To fund the

Terrorist group, among other things, robbed banks. Their biggest score was when they robbed an armored car in Ukiah, California. It netted the homegrown terrorist group 3.6 million dollars. The armored car heist was the biggest news story in the history of Ukiah. News reporters from around the country, including Sacramento's news channels, invaded Ukiah's small town.

The sixteen-year-old *John* and his mother followed "The Order" crime spree on the news and then would have long discussions of their perceived ideals.

THE CRIME SPREE OF "The Order" and the lengthy discussions sparked John's interest in a law enforcement career in John. When John related his plans to put himself through the Sheriff's Academy to his mom at her bedside, contrary to what John had thought her reaction would be, his mom was very supportive. She did, however, make him promise to complete his education and get his degree. She said, "Son, when you become a police officer, I don't want you to stop learning. I want you to take every opportunity they offer to train you to be the best damn cop you can be."

In 1984 John Hunt was sixteen years old, nearly seventeen, the only child of a single mother. His mother worked well beneath her 137 I.Q. as a computer programmer in the basement of Macy's. In 1984 Computer programming on a mainframe using punch cards. John's mom, "Anita Hunt," thought this aspect of her job was mind-numbing as hell, but she knew computers were the future.

John and his mother lived on the fringes of Land Park and Oak Park in Sacramento, California. Their small, simple home was in the grey area of two extremes.

Land Park is a wealthy neighborhood with homes in the millions, with lush green yards manicured every week by a hired gardener. The owners drive luxury cars or large S.U.V.s. Their children go to private schools. And they spend their weekends on trips to Napa Valley to visit their favorite winery estate.

Oak Park is beyond impoverished, with bare dirt for front yards, dogs chained to scraggly trees, rod iron bars on the windows, and old beater cars perched on blocks with the promise of repairs and overrun with gang bangers, pimps, and prostitutes.

When John was twelve years old, the middle school he attended was in the dead center of Oak Park. After school, one of the boys in his class was with a group of older boys. The boy said, "Hey, Wonderbread, what's a cracker like you doin in our school?"

John stood there for a beat. He did the math, eight to one. He had never been in a fight with one boy, let alone eight boys. Some of the boys looked old enough to drive. He took a right turn and headed for home.

All eight of the boys fell in behind John, "Cracker, ain't you gonna answer me? What's a honky like you doin in our school?" John picked up the pace.

He heard the others say, "Yeah honky!" One of the bigger boys shoved John's classmate and said, "kick that mother fucker crackers ass." John glanced over his shoulder to see his classmate charging him. They tumbled head over hill onto the ground. John was being punched in the ribs as they rolled around.

John punched back harder and lower, straight into the kidney. John was getting the upper hand; his classmate was starting to lose with every kidney punch.

The other boys surrounded the two boys on the ground like a pack of wolves. The other boys saw John was winning and started kicking him in the back, in the head, and the ribs. The other boy rolled out of the way, trying not to get kicked. They kept kicking and stomping everywhere. John rolled up into a ball, trying to protect his head. His hands and his fingers broke with one last kick to the head.

The boys took off running, scattering like cockroaches at the sight of a Sacramento P.D. Cruiser a couple of blocks away. When the Sacramento Police Officer notified Anita of what happened, informing her John was at UC Davis medical center for observation. The officer explained the extent of John's injuries. Anita, the love-everyone hippie, lost her bananas. The momma bear came out, and the hippie crap went out the window.

The only positive male role model John had was his Uncle Clarence. Clarence Hunt was the complete polar opposite of his sister. He was a Marine Special Forces S.R.T. operator. When Anita called her brother, she was just this side of hysterical. She said, "I want you to train John not just to protect himself but to kill with his bare fucking hands. He is all I have, and those gang-banging, ghetto-dwelling mother fuckers almost beat him to death." Clarence stifled a chuckle; he had never heard his sister talk this way. She has always been a "Peace and Love" kind of person. He liked his sister's "Momma bear" and agreed to train John to protect himself and bulk John up from his skinny, almost frail frame.

By 1984 John had been training with his Uncle Clarence and working at the same mechanic shop for almost four years. He has always liked wrenching on cars but knew he wanted more out of life. When he was thirteen years old, his mom came home from work to find John in the garage with her car's engine halfway removed. She calmly asked

"John, what are you doing to my car?" John said, "I just wanted to see if I could pull the engine myself." She calmly said, "Okay, when you finish, put it back together." "Thanks, mom," with a big greasy smile.

That same year John completed his first year of general education at Sacramento City College. It is also the year John's mom told him she was ill.

Leading up to his mother's death, if John wasn't at the shop working, he was doing his homework at his mother's bedside. Sometimes, he would just sit with her, talking, as if he wanted to know every detail of her life. John asked questions about her childhood and her parents. She wondered why he had never asked about his father. Sometimes, she would help him with his studies or simply watch television together.

December 1984, the leader of the "The Order," Robert Mathews, was held up in a house on Whidbey Island. Mathews was killed during a shootout with authorities, and the house was engulfed in flames. Mathews became a martyr in the eyes of fellow white nationalists. This same month and year, John's mother succumbed to her illness.

Thirty-four years later, John Hunt retired from his chosen career as a Captain of the El Dorado County Sheriff's Office. During his thirty years with E.D.S.O., he took every opportunity he could to better himself as his mother had wished. By doing so, he followed in Uncle Clarence's footsteps and was part of the Elite S.W.A.T team for most of his career. John trained with the best to be the best.

Don't miss out!

Visit the website below and you can sign up to receive emails whenever Michelle Wishart publishes a new book. There's no charge and no obligation.

https://books2read.com/r/B-A-GGCV-UJICC

BOOKS 2 READ

Connecting independent readers to independent writers.

About the Author

Michelle Wishart is the author of fictional steamy mystery suspense novels. Michelle enjoys spending time with her husband, riding their motorcycles, and documenting their adventures and travels on her YouTube channel, Bells Rides Moto.

Read more at https://bellspublishingco.llc/.

About the Publisher

The owner and founder of Bell's Publishing Co, LLC., Michelle Wishart has a lifelong entrepreneurial spirit. To learn more about Michelle, subscribe to her YouTube channel, "Bells Rides Moto," or Bell's Publishing Co, LLC

Or follow her on Instagram @BellsRide or @BellsPublishingCoLLC